Through the Night

The half-canvassed truck was parked in the middle of the road. In the back was a trestle-table with a wireless receiver standing on it. A long wire aerial swayed above it; and on the roof of the cab a metal ring was turning slowly. Hunched in front of the receiver was a young soldier.

It is over two years since the Nazi invasion of Britain. The villagers of Shevington have been cowed into a sullen acceptance of their new rulers by the horrific reprisals that followed their only attempt at defiance. But someone, somewhere, is still plotting against the oppressors and the Germans have brought in a wireless expert to pinpoint the transmissions so that they can clamp down on this new rebellion before it takes hold.

Frank has never given up hope of finding some way to show the 'Nasties' that they can't have it all their own way, that there are still some people willing to risk everything to fight for freedom—and he has never stopped believing that his father, missing since the invasion, is still alive. The arrival in the village of Stan Crompton, a travelling salesman, brings new danger to Frank and his friends. And, at last, the longed-for chance to fight back. But at what cost . . . ?

Through the Night is a sequel to the acclaimed novel *Against the Day* which was shortlisted for the Angus Book Award.

Michael Cronin is an actor and writer. He has appeared many times on television, on stage, and in films. He is probably best known for *Grange Hill*, where he played Mr Baxter, the gym teacher. He has written two television films, *Stealing the Fire* and *No Final Truth*. *Through the Night* is his second novel for Oxford University Press.

Through the Night

Other books by Michael Cronin

Against the Day

Through the Night

Michael Cronin

OXFORD
UNIVERSITY PRESS

Great Clarendon Street, Oxford OX2 6DP

Oxford University Press is a department of the University of Oxford.
It furthers the University's objective of excellence in research, scholarship,
and education by publishing worldwide in

Oxford New York
Auckland Bangkok Buenos Aires
Cape Town Chennai Dar es Salaam Delhi Hong Kong Istanbul
Karachi Kolkata Kuala Lumpur Madrid Melbourne Mexico City Mumbai
Nairobi São Paulo Shanghai Taipei Tokyo Toronto

Oxford is a registered trade mark of Oxford University Press
in the UK and in certain other countries

First published 2002

British Library Cataloguing in Publication Data available

ISBN 0 19 275221 9

1 3 5 7 9 10 8 6 4 2

Typeset by AFS Image Setters Ltd, Glasgow

Printed in Great Britain
Cox & Wyman Ltd, Reading, Berkshire

For J. C. N.

January 1943

Chapter 1

The snow had stopped but the bruise-coloured sky told them there was more to come.

The wind was still bitter. Still from the East. It seemed to come straight off the Russian steppes and find its way under every gap and loose flap of canvas. There were a dozen of them huddled in the back of the covered lorry, their army greatcoats buttoned up to their chins and their kitbags stacked on the floor at their feet. Soldiers chatting among themselves: recalling the good times they'd had on leave and grimly anticipating their return to duty.

The youngest of them, a slight, fair-haired lad, who sat alone near the back of the truck, said nothing. He'd said very little from the moment he'd climbed aboard. There wasn't much he felt he could say in the company of these campaign-hardened men, some of whom had marched victoriously from Poland to the Atlantic coast of France.

Besides, Dieter Mainz was busy with thoughts of his own. And one or two fears. Not about the posting. No. He was actually looking forward to the challenge his new post, his first post, would involve. Wasn't it true that he'd graduated Best of his Course? But there were one or two things of which he wasn't quite so certain. After all, he had never been out of Germany until early that morning. He had never been further from Dresden, which was his home, than Berlin, which was where he'd attended the Wehrmacht's Signals Training School. And, in a matter of hours, here he was sitting with these veterans bumping along the roads of an occupied country. Although, apart from the snow-bound fields which had rushed up to meet him as the plane dropped out of the clouds, so far all he'd actually seen of his destination had been the inside of the truck.

A loud crack, sharp and precise as a gunshot, made them turn as the canvas at the back of the truck flew open like a loose sail. There were curses; and some of them grabbed for their rifles. But it was only the wind.

It was a moment or two before the canvas could be secured; and peering out into the grey, winter light Dieter thought he caught a glimpse of hills: rolling, long-crested hills rising gently on the left of the narrow road.

'Where are we, sergeant?' he asked.

'You can talk, then?' said the sergeant, who tied off the sheet and sat down opposite him. 'They call it *Sussex*, son. Your first posting, is it?'

Dieter nodded.

'Very nice is *Sussex*.' The sergeant grinned. 'Those hills out there, they're called *the Downs*. Speak any English, do you?'

'Yes, sergeant.' He spoke enough English to know that the sergeant was pulling his leg. Trying to make a fool of him. Those hills could not be called *the Downs* because in English *down* meant . . . He frowned. Well, it certainly did not mean a hill. In English such hills would be called *the Ups*. Still, he wasn't green enough to contradict the sergeant outright.

'*The Downs*, sergeant?' he said. 'That is . . . peculiar.'

The sergeant laughed. '"Peculiar"? It's "peculiar", is it? If you think that's "peculiar" just wait till you meet the people who live there.'

The others laughed.

'Two years I've been stationed in this god-forsaken hole,' said one; 'and I haven't met a man yet who wasn't mad as a dog. They're worse than the French.'

And with that they all began to laugh and stamp their feet noisily on the floor of the truck.

Standing in the shelter of the trees, the two boys watched the truck go by. They might have been thirteen or fourteen years old; but they were bundled up against the cold in such an assortment of ill-fitting clothes it was hard to tell.

The one wearing the man's cap several sizes too big for him shook his head: 'Listen to 'em!'

'Perishin' Nasties!' said his companion. And spat in the snow.

They waited until the truck disappeared along the road and then walked slowly on.

They kept to the edge of the wood, treading carefully where the ground remained clear. The important thing was to move silently and leave no tell-tale tracks. Not that whoever was robbing their snares needed any help; they always seemed to know exactly where to find them.

Beyond the trees the landscape was white and silent. The only sound was the hollow roar of the wind high on the tops of the hills.

It was Frank who saw them first: a set of crisp footprints climbing out of the gully. 'Les!' he whispered.

'What?' And then Les saw them too. 'Oh, no! No,' he said, 'not again!'

They scrambled up the bank and Les began to dig frantically with his fingers. 'It was here,' he said. 'I know it was here!'

'You sure?'

''Course I'm sure; I put it there meself!' He stood up and kicked angrily at the snow. 'It's gone,' he said. 'They've nicked the snare and all! Who'd pull a stunt like that?'

'It's George Poole,' said Frank. 'It's him or Wally Carr. It's bound to be.'

'I ain't so sure.'

There were plenty to choose from. Most of Shevington had been out scavenging these last weeks. People were hungry. And a rabbit, even the stringy, winter kind, could be made to go a long way.

Frank watched his friend kneel, push back his cap, and examine the footprints. It was Les who set the snares each morning. It was Les who knew these woods, the fields, and all the places where the rabbits ran. He knew this countryside inside out. Les Gill, the city boy, was more of a countryman now than most of the village kids.

'That's not Poole,' he said, 'or his nasty pal—that's a man's boot. Let's hope he ain't got to the rest.'

But he had.

'Three of 'em!' Les exclaimed bitterly, as they trudged back towards the village. 'Three good snares!'

'And the rabbit.'

'And the rabbit.'

That was the worst thing. There had been a rabbit in the last snare. But whoever had got there first had taken that too. They'd even had the cheek to stay and gut it before they moved on.

'I'm telling you, Frank, I'm going to pay 'em out for this.'

'We've got to catch 'em first.'

'Don't you worry, I'll catch 'em! See you later.'

Frank Tate watched his friend climb the stile and hurry off across the field. Then he pulled his coat collar closer and started for home.

Home was the cottage he shared with his grandmother, Nan Tate, his aunt Edie Worth, and his cousins, Colin and Rose. The Worths had been at Nan's already when Frank came trudging over the Downs late in the autumn of 1940. Edie and her children had left their home in Swindon that summer after her husband, Len, had been taken prisoner at Dunkirk. Nan's was a small house and a full one. But it was where his father had always told him he must go.

He pushed open the gate and walked round to the back door. He checked the tarpaulin on the old bicycle propped against the wash-house wall. He always did. There was a time when Nan Tate and that bike had been inseparable; not a day had gone by when she wasn't out pedalling the lanes and trackways around Shevington. And all the Jerries' checkpoints and patrols couldn't stop her. Nan Tate, with the picture of Garibaldi above her bed: Garibaldi the Liberator. He lifted the tarpaulin. The rust on the handlebars was getting worse.

She was standing at the bottom of the kitchen garden. She turned and waved as he came down the path. He thought how small she was beginning to look. Small and frail.

'Any luck?' she called.

He shook his head.

'Can't be helped,' she said. 'I know it's not for want of trying.'

'They've been at our traps again.'

'They've what?' Nan struck the ground with her stick. 'What's the matter with people, Frank? Hitler's going to laugh hisself silly when they tell him we're robbing each other! And you can be sure they do.'

'Me and Les'll catch them.'

'And when you do you mind and teach 'em a lesson,' she said. 'Help us indoors.'

He took her arm and they walked slowly up the path together. She stopped near the back door and pointed with her stick to where more tiles had dislodged themselves from the snow-covered roof. 'Ah, Frank!' she sighed. 'It breaks my heart to see the old place looking so shook.'

'I could go up there for you, Nan,' he said. 'If we could borrow a ladder I could sort that out for you.'

'I know. You're a good boy. P'raps come the spring, eh?'

It had been a hard run up from the village and when Colin Worth saw his grandmother and his cousin all he could do was call breathlessly:

'Nan? Frank? Guess what?'

'Colin?'

'Guess what? Just guess what?' he said, hurrying to where they were waiting. 'Go on, guess!'

'What're you talking about, child?'

'Just wait till you hear, Nan. You wait. Nan, he's coming home!'

'Who is?' Nan and Frank looked at each other. 'Who, Colin,' said Nan. 'Who's coming home?'

'They told ma down The Office. Our dad! He's coming home! He's coming home!'

'Len?'

'Yes! She sent me up to tell you. They're going to let some more prisoners of war go free and he's coming home.'

'When?'

'They didn't say. I don't know. It could be any time.' Colin was hopping from one foot to the other with excitement. 'I've got so much to tell him, Nan. Loads. Ma's gone to the pub to tell our Rose. Nan, you and Frank are pleased, aren't you?'

' 'Course we are,' she said. 'Why?'

'Only you looked a bit . . . ' He hesitated. 'You looked a bit . . . you know?'

'Don't be so silly. Go on, you get on back to your mother and sister.'

Frank watched his cousin run back towards the lane. He was full of it, wasn't he? He hadn't even thought how much hungrier they'd all be with another mouth to feed, had he? As though they didn't have enough to . . . He stopped himself. No, that wasn't fair: it wasn't fair to think like that. Yes, but fair or not, these days it was the way things made you think.

'Len Worth coming home at last, eh?' said Nan.

'Looks like it,' he replied.

'Don't take it too hard,' she said. 'Your dad'll come back too, Frank. My Bill'll come back one of these days. We've just got to go on waiting, that's all.'

Frank shrugged. 'I s'pose.'

'Now what d'you mean by that, Frank Tate?'

'I can't help it, Nan. It's hard to keep . . . you know, to keep believing he'll come.'

'He'll come!' said Nan fiercely. 'Don't you ever dare doubt it. You must never give up hope, Frank—not ever, d'you hear?'

'Yes, Nan.'

'Consider Garibaldi!'

'Yes, Nan.'

'And meantime we'll to have to make Len Worth welcome. For Edie's sake, and Colin and Rose. P'raps he can give us a hand with that roof.'

Frank helped her over the worn step into the kitchen and settled her in her chair next to the fire. And then he went upstairs to the boxroom which he and Colin shared.

He pulled his suitcase from under the bed and opened it. There wasn't much inside: a shirt that no longer fitted him, a pair of socks, and one or two photographs. But it wasn't those he was looking for. He slipped his hand into the lining and took out the letter: a single sheet of Red Cross writing-paper which was already beginning to yellow.

> 'Dear Frank,' it began; 'I am writing this in the hope that you are alive and at your nan's. Because of Hitler's birthday they have let the Red Cross come to the camp and said we can write one letter which is this one I'm writing to you, old son . . . '

He didn't read the rest. He knew it by heart:

> 'When they came to Bell's and captured it they wanted me to go on working there but I said no and they arrested me and sent me to . . . ' The German censor had inked out the name of the place ' . . . to work on the big road they're building all the way to . . . ' The censor had inked out that, too. 'Don't worry about me there are plenty a lot worse off. It is hard work but I mean to come through. And

> you must too, old son. You must mean it with all your might. I think of you often. Give my love to your nan and remember me to Edie and her children. This is all the paper they will allow us. I must stop now. I think of you often.
>
> God bless you. Love, Dad.'

His father was alive. At least, he was in the spring of 1941 when the letter was written. There had been no word since. His father's voice was getting fainter. And the dreams, those once frequent dreams, dreams that were so real, in which Bill Tate came striding up the lane to Nan's gate, dreams from which Frank always woke so full of hope, they were rarer now.

He looked up. Outside the window the snow had begun to fall again. And downstairs he could hear his aunt Edie singing.

Chapter 2

The clerk behind the desk scooped the contents of his pencil-sharpener into a neat pile.

'There will be coal,' he said.

'But when? The children can't learn if they're frozen stiff. How many times . . . ' Words deserted Peter Sims and the young teacher ran his fingers nervously through his thinning hair. 'Surely the school is a priority?'

The queue waited patiently. And from the wall above them the portrait of the Führer, Adolf Hitler, glared down implacably. The *'BKVZ'*—The Bureau for the Control and Administration of Civilian Affairs—had replaced the old Checkpoint which had stood on the north side of Shevington Green. The endless stream of rules and regulations which issued from the busy, wooden building controlled the lives of the villagers far more effectively than the striped barrier and sentry-box had ever done. There was never a time of day when there wasn't a queue inside and outside 'The Office'.

'I've had to send my pupils home three days running,' said Sims. And suddenly threw his hat down on the counter. 'Did you hear what I said?'

'The coal will come,' said the clerk calmly. And brushed the scattered pencil-shavings into the waste-paper basket.

Peter Sims snatched up his hat and hurried to the door.

Mildred Gill looked up as he went by. There was only one woman between her and the desk now. It wouldn't be long.

She went back to her book. Nowadays, when you had

to queue for just about everything, when everyone seemed to spend most of their lives waiting for something or the other, Mill Gill always took a book with her. It was Vera who'd suggested she did that. It was Vera who had taught her to read. Vera Thrale had taught her so many things. People thought Vera was a bit odd but she wasn't—Vera made things make sense. Even the oddest things.

'Next!'

To Mill's surprise the new ration books were stamped and waiting. 'Wonders'll never cease!' she said.

The clerk looked up at her. 'This means?'

'Nuffin',' she replied.

As she left she smiled at the others who were waiting but no one spoke or returned her smile. The village had never taken to Mildred and her brother. 'Those cockneys' would always be outsiders. Because of where they were from, the way they spoke, what people thought they were. But she and Les weren't what people thought they were. That was another thing Vera had taught Mill: a lot of people weren't what people thought they were.

Mill and Les Gill had come a long way from the two bug-ridden rooms in Bermondsey they had once called home. It was an awful thing to say, she thought, but the war had given them a lot to be grateful for. 'Course, she and Les had always had each other. It was about all they did have. But being taken in by the Thrales, Vera and Alec, had changed their lives. Completely. Hadn't it just! When she thought what their life had been like! When she thought how different things had been before that! When she thought . . . No! Mill shook her head. 'No, I ain't going to remember any of that,' she said. 'Cos it ain't worth the effort.'

She crossed The Green and started up the lane towards Thrales'. As she walked she opened her book again. Vera had loads of books. This one was *A Tale of Two Cities*. By Charles Dickens. And it was a bit sad. Poor souls—you had to feel sorry for them. She was trying to find her place when she caught sight of the hunched figure sheltering against the hedge. It was a Jerry soldier. A young one. He was trying to light a cigarette. His face was turned away but as she approached he looked up and saw her. He smiled sheepishly.

'Who're *you* lookin' at?' she said.

'Looking at?'

'I saw you.'

'I do not understand,' he said. And came towards her.

She stepped back quickly, holding her book in front of her like a shield. 'Don't you try nuffin'!'

'I am trying to light my cigarette, that is all. You misunderstand.'

'No, I don't,' she said.

'And I am walking along the road. May I know if it is unacceptable?'

'Do what?' She suddenly laughed. She couldn't help herself.

'You are laughing at me?' he said.

'Cos you sound funny,' she said. 'Why do Jerries sound like toffs when they talk English?'

'Toffs?'

'All pound-note-ish. You sound like a proper gent—a gentleman.'

'Oh, no!' He shook his head vehemently. 'I am not a gentleman.'

'Aincha? I've been warned about men like you,' she said. And laughed again. 'So what are you, then?'

'A corporal.' He proudly tapped the chevron stripe on his field-grey sleeve.

'And what's that other badge?' she asked.

'I am a member of the Signals Corps. I am . . . I am a wireless operator.'

'En't you sure?'

'Yes, I am sure.'

'Is that how come you talk English?'

'I have learned to do so quite recently,' he said proudly. 'Before I was posted to England. I am here only one week.' He took out a packet of Wehrmacht-issue cigarettes. 'Do you care to smoke?'

Oh, she did care! Whenever possible. Which wasn't often these days. Tobacco was hard to come by.

'Take one. Or two,' said the soldier. 'I have plenty of them.'

'Nah,' she said, 'I better not.'

'But why not?'

'Because—that's why.' She hesitated. He wasn't much in his baggy uniform. She could make two of him. But he had nice eyes. Greyish. And kind-looking.

'May I ask how old are you?' he said.

'Me? Seventeen,' she said. ''Bout the same as you.'

'Oh, no!' he replied indignantly. 'I am a little older.'

'Not much you ain't! Anyway,' she said, 'I've got to go. I can't hang about chewin' the fat with you all afternoon.'

'Young lady? If you please, my name is Dieter Mainz. What is your name?'

'None of your business. But if you must know it's Mill,' she said and walked away.

'Mill?'

'That's right.'

'Ah—Millicent!'

She turned and looked back to where he was standing. 'Do what?'

'Millicent? That is your name?'

He was smiling. Ever so nicely. 'Millicent? Yeah,' she said. 'Yeah, Millicent, that's right.'

Alec Thrale withdrew to his work-shed most afternoons. He would sit for hours among his redundant traps and tools, smoking an occasional pipe of the tobacco his resourceful wife had dried and blended from the herb patch in the garden beyond.

Keeper Thrale had walked the covers of Shevington Hall, man and boy, as long as he could remember; and his father had walked them before him. But after 'the terrorist incident' General von Schreier had had no choice but to dismiss all civilian staff from his headquarters. Or so he said. For Alec to see his life's work abandoned, his pheasant pens left to the fox, and the woods he loved felled and trampled over by German patrols, was a bitter blow. But one which, somewhat to his wife's surprise, the keeper seemed to bear with remarkable equanimity.

'Alec, dear?'

He looked up to find her standing in the doorway. 'What's that, Vera?'

'I've searched the cellar from top to bottom but I can't find the other hurricane-lamp.'

'We've hardly enough paraffin for them we've got.'

'But some more light would make such a difference to these gloomy evenings.'

'All right. I'll have a look for it after tea,' he said.

'Thank you, dear.'

He sat for a while after she'd gone, finishing his pipe. Then he got up and lifted down one of the sickles from the wall. Taking his sharpening-stone he began to edge the blade with long, careful strokes.

He liked to keep his tools in good order. The way he kept the garden and the cottage and everything else in good order. And with Vera's industrious housekeeping and ingenuity the four of them, Alec, Vera, Mildred, and Leslie, survived. They went without, certainly—like everyone else—but they survived. You couldn't ask to do much more than that. Not in times like these.

However, throughout the winter months there was little for Alec to do other than plan the work the spring would require. And to sit. And remember, of course. Like most people in those dark days he did plenty of that.

And it was Ted Naylor who, more often than not, seemed to come to mind. Ted the poacher. Aye, and a good poacher too. Credit where it was due. Even though that bomb of his had cost them all their jobs up at the Hall. Ted had fought back. He'd bloodied the Jerries' noses for them! By God, he had! But the retribution that followed had been brutal, the reprisals merciless. Losing jobs didn't amount to much in comparison to what some people had had to suffer. People had been taught a terrible lesson. And now they were . . . They were what? Hangdog, cowed, that's what they were. Though, truth to tell, it was hard to blame them.

When Les came in and slumped down on the upturned box opposite Alec knew it had happened again.

'Snares and all?' he said.

Les nodded. 'Just like last time.'

'They'd take the bread from a babby's fist some of the blighters would!'

'I've got to catch 'em, Mr Thrale.'

'And mind you take a stout stick with you.'

Alec always had an answer. And when he hadn't he told you so. And he told you things quietly, not like he was telling you anything at all; chatting on in that deliberate way he had, explaining things, making you see how important things were. Les had learned so much from the keeper almost without knowing it.

He watched him get up and replace the sickle on the wall; and saw him hesitate, as he always did, beside the empty gun-rack.

'The Jerries never did give your shotgun back, did they, Mr Thrale?' he said.

'No, Leslie,' said the keeper, 'no, they never did. That gun meant a lot to me.'

'What did it mean to you, Mr Thrale?'

The keeper shook his head. 'It's hard to find the words for a thing like that, Leslie,' he said. 'Because it's a thing about yourself, you see? A private thing. Some things are like that. But I can remember the day my father give me that gun. I can remember that day as plain as you like.'

'I bet if you was to go and ask the General for it back . . . '

'Ask von Schreier? This cold weather's got to your brain, boy!'

'He's s'posed to be a gent,' said Les.

'He might be what Hitler and his pals call a gent; here we call them bloody murderers.'

'But he's a soldier, Mr Thrale. That's what soldiers do, don't they? Kill people, I mean.'

'Like what they done to Middelbury? Like what they done to Ted Naylor's village?'

'No,' said Les quickly. 'No, 'course not.'

'That was done on von Schreier's orders and don't you ever forget it, d'you hear?'

'No, Mr Thrale.'

'Well?'

'Nothing.'

'You looked like you was going to say something else.'

Les shook his head. He had his own reasons for remembering Ted Naylor. Reasons he had often wanted to share with the man standing opposite. There'd been so many times when he'd almost told him. But a secret was a secret.

Alec took his watch from his waistcoat pocket and flipped it open. Then he walked out into the yard and Les followed.

Keeper's Cottage had been built at the edge of the woods which surrounded Shevington Hall. But there was now a dense tangle of barbed-wire separating it from the trees. As Thrale and Les emerged from the shed, one of the regular patrols went past on the other side of the wire: two armed soldiers and a large Alsatian dog.

When they had gone, Alec remained for a while peering into the trees and undergrowth beyond. Then: 'She'll have a bit of tea ready by now,' he said. 'We'd better go in.'

As they were walking back towards the house Mill appeared from the direction of the lane. Alec went inside but Les waited for her. Despite the failing light she had her head in a book. She was often like that these days, he thought. Miles away. She didn't hear a thing you said to her.

'Know what?' he said. And she looked up in surprise.

‘’Lo, Les,’ she said.

‘Know what, Mill? One of these days you’ll be reading like that and you’re going to fall down a bloody great hole!’

Frank Tate stamped the snow from his shoes. ‘Nan?’ he called and pushed open the kitchen door. ‘I’ve been to see Farmer Follett.’

They were all there: his aunt Edie, Colin, Rose, and Nan in her favourite chair. And sitting at the table with a plate in front of him was a thin-looking man with a pale, unshaven face.

‘Frank,’ said his aunt, ‘this is your uncle Len.’

‘It’s our dad,’ said Colin. And placed an arm around his father’s shoulder. ‘Isn’t it, Dad?’

‘He got a lift,’ said Edie. ‘He caught us all on the hop. Did you want another slice of bread, Len?’

Len Worth nodded without looking up from his plate.

He didn’t look like a soldier, thought Frank. He had no uniform. And the threadbare, civilian clothes he was wearing didn’t fit: he looked like a tramp.

‘John Follett, did you say, Frank?’ said Nan.

‘Yes, Nan. I went to see him about a ladder. To sort out those tiles,’ he replied. ‘He asked to be remembered to you.’

‘That was kind of him.’

‘Frank is our Bill’s boy, Len,’ said Edith. ‘You remember my brother Bill?’

‘I remember him,’ said Len, wiping his plate with the slice of bread. He looked across at Frank. ‘He’s got his father’s eyes,’ he said. ‘That’s the way Bill Tate used to look at people. Wary looking.’

‘Be fair, Len,’ said Nan. ‘The boy’s never seen you before. You’re a stranger.’

‘Oh, mother, don’t say it like that,’ said Edie.

‘It’s only the truth, girl.’

‘Is that what I am?’ Len pushed away the plate and

stood up. 'I'm a stranger, am I?' He snatched up the muddy greatcoat from the chair beside him and started to pull it on.

'Len!' Edie took hold of his sleeve.

'If I'm not welcome here, Edie, I'll go elsewhere.'

'Len, sit down, do,' said Nan. 'You're more than welcome, you know that. Edie, squeeze the pot and we'll all have another cup of tea. Len, sit down. Please.'

Len did sit down. But he didn't take his coat off. He sat at the table waiting to catch the eye of anyone who looked his way. But no one did.

Colin hurriedly heaped some more wood on the fire. And Rose reached her mac and headscarf down from behind the door.

'I'd better be off,' she said. 'Mr Poole will be wondering where I've got to. Cheerio, Dad. I'll see you later, eh? Come down the Shevvy and have a pint.'

'Where are you going?'

'To work.'

'Work?'

'At the Shevvy, The Shevington Arms,' she said.

'A public house?' Len turned to Edie. 'Good God, woman, what's she doing working in a public house?'

'Oh, Len, there's no shame involved. People take work wherever they can these days.'

'She's a good girl, Len,' said Nan. 'I don't know what we'd have done without the bit of money she brings home.'

'You're welcome to your opinion, Mrs Tate,' replied Len. 'But I think I know what's right and proper where my own flesh and blood are concerned.'

'I daresay you do, Len,' said Nan. 'But there's been a change or two since you went away. It might be as well to remember that. How's the tea coming along, Edie?'

But Edie didn't seem to be listening. 'You must be dog-tired, Len,' she said. 'Why don't you go up and have a lie down, eh?'

Len Worth drew his hand across his face. 'Tired ain't the half of it,' he said.

'He came all the way from Dover,' said Colin when they'd gone. 'That's where the ship landed him early this morning. I'm going to ask him about the war when he wakes up. And what it's like in France. And . . . '

'Just give your father some time to himself, Colin,' said Nan. 'I daresay he's a bit overwhelmed with it all.'

'Yes, Nan.'

'And you get off to work, Rose, or you'll be late. Don't take it to heart, girl. He'll get used to us. Everything's bound to be a shock for him.'

'It don't matter, Nan.' Colin sighed. 'Cos it'll be all right now. Now our dad's home things'll be all right.'

Peter Sims shook the snow from his brolly and slipped his key into the lock.

He let himself in and stood listening at the foot of the stairs. There had been no furious barking to greet him and all the lights were out. His landladies, the two Miss Elliotts, and their excitable terrier, Ilkley, must have gone visiting. He had to confess he was relieved. Oh, the ladies were cheerful enough creatures; and their generosity and welcome had never faltered despite the increasing hardships they were all forced to share. But there were times when a little peace and quiet was the most welcome thing of all. After a long and difficult day, and an afternoon wasted making a fool of himself in front of the queue at The Office, what the acting-Headmaster of Shevington School wanted most were the consolations of his sitting room and his chair beside the fire.

He took off his hat and slowly climbed the stairs. He noticed again how threadbare the carpet had begun to look. Like so much else. The world, he reflected, had become an altogether shabbier place. For all their uniforms and flags, for all their posturing and noisy certainties, what the Nazis had actually brought was shabbiness.

'Good Lord!' He reached nervously for the banister to

steady himself. There, distinctly visible under his door, was a thin line of light!

Had he forgotten to turn it off when he went out that morning? Surely not? Electricity was at a premium and he was a stickler in these matters.

'Yes?' he called nervously. And then: 'Is there . . . is there anyone there?'

For a moment there was no reply. But then the door to his room was opened and a short, stocky figure in an overcoat and muffler appeared on the landing.

'Ah, there you are, old man!' he said. 'You must be Sims.'

'Who . . . who are you? What are you . . . ?'

'Crompton's the name, Stanley Crompton. Just having a look round.'

'In my room?'

'No need for offence, I hope? You know how it is with new diggings. Mind you, truth to tell, the room the ladies have put me in couldn't be more suitable. Funny old ducks, aren't they? Do come up.'

'Am I to understand that you are lodging here?'

'Hole in one, old man! They told me in the village shop that the ladies might have room for a little 'un. So here I am! I'm just across the landing.' Stanley Crompton stood back as Mr Sims went past and then followed him in. 'I must say you've made this a proper home from home,' he said. 'Not to my taste, of course. A few too many books for my money! More like a blessed library than a sitting room! But, then, the ladies tell me you're something of a scholar. Up at the varsity and all that, eh?' Crompton pointed to the photograph on the wall beside the bookshelf: a group of young men in academic gowns standing together on a summer's day beside a river. 'Here,' he said, 'I don't s'pose you ever rowed in the Boat Race?'

'No,' said Sims, 'I did not.' He was beginning to recover himself. 'Now, if you'll excuse me, I've had rather a difficult day.'

'It's been a pig, hasn't it! I've been driving round this perishin' countryside for hours! Selling's my game. Brushes. Bit of a joke at a time like this. Still, life goes on. And dust is always with us. At least, it is as long as you're not using a Dust-Well Full Domestic. But I can see I'm keeping you. And I'm sure there'll be plenty of opportunities for a proper chinwag. Perhaps we can take a glass of ale together one evening?'

'I'm afraid my evenings are fully occupied . . . '

' 'Struth!'

'What is it?'

Crompton had stopped by the table on which were spread a large map, some notebooks, and a selection of photographs of what looked like a ruined building. 'That looks nasty!' he exclaimed.

'What do you mean?'

'Took a direct hit, did it?'

'A direct hit? Certainly not!' said Sims. 'That is Patfield Palace: the Roman villa on the Patfield Road.'

'Getaway?'

'I'm preparing a paper on . . . on its importance.'

'Oh, I say! Well, each to his own. Goodnight then, Professor. And very nice to have met you.'

As the door closed Mr Sims collapsed into a chair.

What an appalling little man!

Chapter 3

These days it was rare to see a civilian vehicle on the road. Petrol was in short supply. But Frank had seen this one several times in the last few days.

This morning it was parked at the entrance to one of the fields next to the lane. The driver was standing beside it. He had unfolded a map on the bonnet and was studying it intently.

'All right, mister?' said Frank, as he drew level.

The traveller looked up. 'What's that, old man?'

'Are you lost?'

'As a matter of fact, I think I am,' he said, closing the map quickly. 'It's all a bit hit and miss without the signposts, isn't it?'

The signposts around the village, like everywhere else, had been taken down when invasion seemed imminent. Most of them had never been replaced. There were the military signs, of course, directing traffic to the Wehrmacht's Southern Area Command Headquarters at Shevington Hall. They were everywhere. But they were all in German.

'What are you looking for?' asked Frank.

'Looking for? Shevington.'

'Shevington? But Shevington's at the bottom of the lane.'

'Is it? Well, I'm blessed; I really do seem to have lost my sense of direction. You must think I'm all sorts of a fool.'

That was just what Frank did think but it wasn't good manners to tell him so. Besides, there might be a lift on offer. And a ride in a car wasn't a treat you came by every day of the week. 'Easy enough,' he said, 'if you're a stranger. Matter of fact, I'm going that way.'

But the motorist didn't bite. He nodded abstractedly and tucked the map into his pocket. 'Much obliged,' he said.

Stingy perisher! thought Frank, as he walked on down the lane. He hadn't gone far when he heard the car starting up. But, for some reason, the driver must have changed his mind because it never came past him.

Nan insisted that Frank turn up for school each morning. But Les seemed to bother less and less. It was odd not having Les around. He missed his company. And he missed not having him there to help see off George Poole and the rest of the village kids. Still, it was only a matter of months now before they'd both be old enough to leave altogether.

Mr Sims was standing at the top of the steps when Frank arrived. 'I'm sorry, Tate,' he said. 'We've had to cancel lessons yet again.'

'Couldn't I collect some wood or something,' said Frank. 'I could make up the boiler and keep an eye on it. There must be something I can do.'

'I'm afraid there isn't much any of us can do, Tate.' The teacher took off his spectacles and wiped them wearily on his handkerchief. 'You'd best get along home.'

Frank crossed the empty playground and sat on the churchyard wall. He watched Mr Sims go back inside and then saw him reappear and stand at the window of his office. And he wondered what the teacher might be thinking.

Does he ever remember? he wondered. Or am I the only one? After all, Mr Sims never mentions it. And Les? He never mentions it either.

Was he the only one who still remembered the day they brought the bomb from Seabourne to Shevington?

Frank and his dad had been living at The White Horse Inn, the guest-house in Seabourne, throughout the summer of 1940. Seabourne with its boarded shops and deserted hotels; the coiled barbed-wire guarding the Promenade; the tank-traps crowding the pebbles below; and the waiting, grey Channel waters. On the September night when Hitler's armies had stormed ashore all along the south coast, Frank's father had been fire-watching, taking his turn at the factory where he worked on the outskirts of the town. But when the fighting was over Bill Tate had not come home.

That's what Frank and Les had been doing there that day all those months later. Looking for something, anything, that might explain what had happened to his dad. And they'd tried. At Bell's Engineering. At the Town Hall. But they'd found nothing. Well, nothing that didn't simply add to the mystery. But what they had found, to their surprise, hurrying along the Prom, was Mr Sims and his basket. The basket which turned out to contain the makings of Ted Naylor's bomb.

Was he the only one who still remembered that day? That incredible day and the days that followed? Didn't anyone else remember the excitement they'd all felt? And the hope? The discovery that you could do it, that you could fight back, had been like a light coming on suddenly in a darkened room. Or the blaze from one of those beacons you read about, one of those they lit when the Spanish Armada was sighted, sending the call to arms from hilltop to hilltop. But Ted Naylor's flame had flickered only briefly. The world was an even darker place now. Oh, what was the matter with people! You'd think they were the ones in the wrong, not the perishing Nasties!

Their footsteps echoed on the marble stairs as General Klaus von Schreier and his personal aide, Oberleutnant Werner Lang, made their way to the Great Reception Room on the first floor of Shevington Hall.

When they reached the landing the General paused by

the window. The grounds of the Hall lay spread out below. The gravel paths of the Knot Garden had been cleared and were etched darkly against the snow. Beyond the garden was a no-man's land where the ancient woods had been felled for half a mile in every direction. That, reflected the General, had been a regrettable necessity. But the repairs to the long windows overlooking the terrace were still evident even two years later. One terrorist and a small bomb had caused a great deal of damage. And trouble. One terrorist? No. There were accomplices, of course. There always were. Indeed, the Gestapo had assured him that this must be the case. They had also assured him that those accomplices would be caught no matter how long it took. The Gestapo never closed its files. The punitive measures the General had imposed after the attack on the Hall had been yet another regrettable necessity. They had been particularly rigorous. But they had been effective. There had been no further incidents. None the less, constant vigilance was required. Look away, stop listening, even for a moment and the reward could be an invitation to the *Bal Russe*: a one-way ticket to the Tea Dance at Stalingrad or some other chilly venue along the Eastern Front.

Oberleutnant Lang waited. He had been aide to the General since the invasion of Poland in '39. They had marched a long way together. And Werner Lang knew the General very well. And he knew—though he was far too loyal to have admitted it to anyone else—that General Klaus von Schreier was bored. He was removing himself more and more from the everyday chores the Occupation demanded. He seemed to spend more and more time closeted in the Library, bunkered behind his beloved books. Still, this afternoon it had been the General's own decision to visit the Communications Room.

Von Schreier turned away from the window. 'Well, Werner,' he said, 'shall we see what our expert has for us?'

'Herr General.' The Oberleutnant reached for the handle and pushed open the tall, panelled doors.

Von Schreier surveyed the rows of tables and cabinets of electronic equipment stacked around the walls of the elegant, eighteenth-century room. Shevington Hall was one of the nerve centres of the Wehrmacht's Southern Area Communications System, a network which stretched from Dover in the east to Devon in the west. These transmitters and receivers were manned twenty-four hours a day, monitoring and broadcasting a constant traffic of commands, information, and intelligence. And yet it was the silence of the room that always astonished the General: no sound other than a steady, eerie hum, and the occasional irritable rattle of a Morse key.

A young man sitting slightly apart from the rest removed his headphones as the two officers approached his position.

'Stand easy, Mainz,' said the Oberleutnant. 'Signals Corporal Mainz is our new ears for any illicit transmissions the terrorists may attempt, Herr General.'

The General nodded. In the last month there had been several reports of unauthorized transmissions in his sector. They were rare but that they were happening at all caused the General concern. Which was why he had asked Berlin to send him a specialist. And was this the best they could offer? A boy? 'You have been with us how long, Mainz?' he enquired.

'Two weeks, Herr General. Since I came from the training school.'

'An "expert" fresh from training-school, eh, Werner?'

'Quite so, Herr General. Make your report, Mainz.'

'I am maintaining watch on the frequencies provided by the panoramic monitoring centres in both Paris and Berlin, Herr General.'

'These transmissions have occurred over a wide area of our sector, Mainz. Do you think this means there is more than one operator at work?'

'Possibly, Herr General.'

'Possibly? You can be no more precise?'

'The locations were calculated on information provided by the goniometric bases in Brest, Augsburg, and Nuremberg, which—'

'Never mind the lecture, Mainz. I want to know how close you can bring us to this terrorist.'

'The most recent tracing produced a triangle with sides of fifteen kilometres in the west of the sector, Herr General. The illegal was somewhere inside that triangle. We must now wait for another transmission.'

'And then?'

'As soon as Paris or Berlin notify me of the wavelength he is using I will be able to reduce the triangle.'

'Do so, Mainz. I want him located. And then we can hand the whole thing over to the Gestapo,' said the General. 'I'm relying on you, Mainz,' he called, as he walked away between the tables.

The corporal saluted: 'I will find him, Herr General.'

He settled back in his chair and glanced around the room. Well, at least now they would all see that he was being taken seriously. The 'expert' had already become something of a joke. The other operators had begun to cup a hand to their ears as he passed and call: 'Is there anybody there?'

There was somebody there. Paris with its tracing screens for the whole of Europe had said so. So had Berlin. And Dieter Mainz was going to find out who it was.

He pulled on his headphones. Another hour or so on listening-duty and then, during his break, he thought he might take another walk along the lane.

Peter Sims removed his spectacles and looked at his watch. It was gone three o'clock! How the time had flown by! Yes, keeping busy was always the answer. Relaxing, letting your mind dwell on things, was to be avoided at all costs. That way lay despair. Occupied! That was the thing to be.

He closed the manuscript before him and looked again at the title-page:

'A Comprehensive Appraisal
of the Roman Villa and Outbuildings
known as Patfield Palace
at Patfield, West Sussex.'

It was Henry Underwood who had begun to excavate the neglected ruins not long before the outbreak of war. Henry, the previous headmaster's only son, had been killed in one of the great tank battles which had rolled back and forth across the Midlands in the bitterly fought days before the Surrender. And it was to Peter Sims Henry's father had entrusted his son's notebooks and photographs to edit and assemble into a tribute to him.

The ancient walls and scattered stones which lay either side of the Patfield Road had been known as The Palace since time immemorial. Most local people assumed that the name was a joke. But Henry Underwood had been convinced that it wasn't a joke at all. And his notebooks endeavoured to prove it. Patfield Palace, he argued, was the palatial home of some exceptionally wealthy Romano-Briton. But his argument needed more proof, more researching. For almost two years Peter Sims had spent countless long, but never lonely, evenings poring over every reference book he could lay his hands on. Books crammed with plans and pictures of the great villas and palaces of Ancient Rome. Elegant country retreats and ostentatious palaces—like the seaside splendours along the bay at Baiae! Buildings of elaborate grandeur with peristyle gardens, colonnaded façades, and porticoes and podia so grand that they often concealed a complete underground corridor of their own—a cryptoporticus!

Sims sighed: ah, but where was the proof that Patfield was part of such glories? Other than that wonderful and almost perfectly preserved mosaic, the Proserpina Floor, Patfield refused to yield any evidence that it was anything more than an extensive domestic dwelling—a farm. A wealthy one but a farm and probably no more than that. But Peter Sims went on looking. The looking was all.

The door of his office opened and his assistant, Audrey Meacher, came in.

'Always at work, Mr Sims! I do admire the way you manage to keep yourself so busy,' she said.

He smiled. 'One makes an effort, you know.'

She thought how weary he looked. It was a thankless task trying to keep the school going against all the odds. With the authorities in no hurry to consider the needs of a small village school like theirs Mr Sims had had very little choice about stepping into old Mr Underwood's shoes when he retired. Filling them, of course, was quite another matter.

'I hope you won't think me unduly personal, Mr Sims,' she said, 'but you do look awfully tired.'

'Thank you, Miss Meacher.'

'Forgive me, I didn't mean to be rude.'

'Not at all. It was kind of you to remark. As a matter of fact, I haven't been sleeping properly.'

'Is it this ridiculous situation with the fuel supply?'

'Partially. Although, to be perfectly honest, it's more to do with the awful man who's staying at my digs.'

'I didn't know you had a fellow guest.'

'Since the beginning of the week. His name's Crompton. He's a salesman.' Sims shook his head. 'He's quite relentless. He comes into my room in the evening and just chatters on and on. He kept me up till all hours last night. And it's all the most extraordinary nonsense. The same silly questions over and over again.'

'Questions?'

'Oh, yes. His curiosity is positively voracious. I can't imagine why he expects me to know everything about the village. I realize a salesman needs to know all he can about potential customers but . . . '

'But what, Mr Sims?'

'I don't know. There really is something not quite right about him.'

'Oh, dear.'

'What is it, Miss Meacher?'

'It's just that . . . I hesitate to . . . '

'Yes?'

'I know one is inclined to imagine only the worst in these awful times but . . . look here, you don't suppose he's a German stooge, do you?'

'Good heavens, Miss Meacher, I think that's a little fanciful.'

'I assure you that is the expression. And you did say he's always asking questions. After all, that's the way they do it, isn't it? That's how the Nazis find out things about us.'

'You mean . . . '

'It is, isn't it?'

'Yes. Yes, it is but . . . ' Sims ran his fingers nervously through his hair. 'No. No,' he said, 'I think Mr Crompton has a rather "commercial" manner, that's all.'

In winter, curfew began at nine o'clock in the evening and was only lifted again an hour before dawn. Between those times, to be discovered outside without official permission meant immediate arrest. Or worse.

The fact that his customers had to be home and behind doors so early each evening was a source of irritation and concern for Harry Poole, the landlord of The Shevington Arms. And, each evening, as the hands of the clock above the bar moved towards the time they would all rise and hurry out into the night, he became visibly desperate to obtain one last round of orders from the smoke-filled room.

'Start collecting any empties, girl,' he observed to Rose Worth not long after quarter past eight. 'It makes 'em look at the clock. You know the routine.'

'Right ho, Mr Poole,' she replied.

He watched her make her way between the tables. She was a pretty girl. Cheerful, too. She brightened the place up, there was no question of that. But if things went on the way they were going he'd have to get rid of her. Times were hard and getting harder. If he had had to depend solely on the beer he sold Harry Poole's prospects would have looked very dire indeed. But Harry had one or two other irons in the fire. Only that morning he'd received a consignment of sugar from one of the cooks with whom he had an arrangement up at the Hall. Sugar, cigarettes, even a little butter from time to time found their way into Harry Poole's storeroom; and from there, at a price, to a few select shelves elsewhere in the district.

Rose stopped when she came to the table by the door. 'All right, Phil?' she asked.

The young man who stood watching the cribbage-players looked back at her and smiled. 'Always the better for seeing you, Rose,' he said.

'You go on!' she laughed.

'Have you had a chance to speak to your ma?' he said confidentially.

'Not yet,' she said.

And she was about to say more when the door behind them opened. There was a barrage of angry shouts as the cold air rushed in and the new arrival quickly closed it behind him. It was Mr Dearman, who ran the village shop.

'Well, I'm blessed—here's a turn-up!' exclaimed Harry Poole, as everyone turned to stare at the shopkeeper. Mr Dearman was staunchly teetotal and had never been known to set foot in the pub. 'Driven you to drink at last, has it, Mr D.?'

There was some laughter but the shopkeeper shook his head gravely.

'There's been a shooting,' he said.

'Do what?'

'There's been a shooting. I've come to warn everybody.'

'What d'you mean?' 'Where?' came a chorus of voices. 'Who?' 'Who's been shot?'

'Young Ned Follett,' he replied. 'Out at his father's place. It was one of their patrols. They challenged him and he didn't answer. He started to run and they shot at him.'

'He's only a kid.'

'They shot him just the same.'

'Dead, d'you mean?'

The shopkeeper shook his head. 'No, thank the Lord. But he's hurt badly. They've taken him to the cottage hospital. I thought people should know so they can get home and inside. The Germans will be jumpy after this. Goodnight to you all.'

There was silence as the door closed behind the shopkeeper. Then a burst of noisy conversation as everyone spoke at once:

'He ain't no more than eight or nine!'

' 'Tisn't as though it's curfew or anything!'

'Shooting children, is that what it's come to?'

'They've always had it in for the Folletts,' observed the elderly man in the chair nearest the fire.

'How d'you mean?'

The old man tapped his nose. 'John Follett was the last person to see Ted,' he said cryptically.

'They've been biding their time to pay 'im back ever since,' said someone else.

The conversation died for a second or two. Until a voice said quietly: 'We could do with a few more Ted Naylors, if you ask me.'

'Ah,' said another, 'Ted showed the blighters what for.'

'He give 'em a taste of their own medicine.'

'That's all they understand.'

'Now hold your horses—just hold your horses!' said Harry Poole banging on the counter. 'That's enough of that sort of talk. Let's be careful what's being said, if you please.'

'And what's that supposed to mean?'

'What I said. I don't want my pub getting a reputation

for loose talk. They'd take any excuse to close us down good and proper. And then where would you all go of an evening, eh?'

The old man by the fire stood up and pushed away his chair. 'You can stop us talking, Harry Poole,' he said, 'but you can't stop us remembering.'

The pub began to empty quickly as the drinkers drained their glasses, pulled on their coats, and hurried out into the night.

Among them was Stan Crompton, who, before he left, returned his glass to the bar. He smiled at Harry Poole: 'Quite right too, old man,' he said. 'You can never be too careful.'

'Thank you, Mr Crompton,' said Poole. 'I'm glad there's someone here with half an ounce of sense.'

'Would that be the Follett with the farm a mile or two beyond the Hall they were talking about?'

'John Follett, that's right. Do you know him?'

'Not personally,' said the traveller, buttoning his coat. 'But he's on my list.'

Harry Poole frowned. And, for some reason, found himself thinking about that sugar hidden in his storeroom. 'How d'you mean?' he said.

Stan Crompton laughed: 'You're all on my list, Mr Poole. Everybody's got some dust under their table, haven't they? Goodnight to you. And you, miss.'

'I thought our dad might have looked in tonight,' said Rose Worth, as she and Phil Gingell made their way up the lane. 'It'd really do him good. Phil?'

'Sorry, Rose,' he replied. 'I was miles away. Thinking about Ned Follett.'

'Poor little mite.'

'And I was thinking how we was there that night; you know, at the dance in Follett's barn the night Ted Naylor . . . remember?'

''Course I do,' she said, squeezing his arm. 'That's where we met.'

'He was a hero, no question.'

'Phil, you wouldn't get mixed up in anything like that, would you?' she said anxiously. 'I couldn't bear for you to be killed like Ted Naylor.'

'That's all over, Rose. There ain't much likelihood of that. Listen, how come you haven't spoke to your mother yet?'

'I can't, Phil—not yet, eh? She'll be bound to try and put the damper on it. Can't we keep it a secret a bit longer? I just want to be happy for the minute. There'll be plenty of old miseries who'll want to put the kibosh on it. But I ain't going to let them. Oh, Phil, people can't just not go on, can they? You've got to go on living. Cos that's what life does. Go on, I mean.'

He smiled. 'Know what you are, Rose Worth?' he said. 'You're a proper tonic!' And kissed her.

Chapter 4

'It's no good, Les,' said Frank, 'I've got to stand up.' He stretched his arms painfully. 'What d'you reckon the time is?'

Les glanced up at the pale sun which was beginning to dip below the tops of the trees. 'It's getting on,' he said. 'They've got to come soon.'

The wood was quiet. Occasionally the wind rattled a dead leaf or set a bare branch creaking above them but that was all. They'd been hidden deep in the holly since the middle of the afternoon. As the sun went down the rabbits would emerge. And so might the thief.

'It can't get much colder, can it?' said Frank.

'Stick some newspaper up your shirt, like I do,' said Les.

'Newspaper?'

'Yes. It keeps you warm. That was Vera come up with that idea.'

'Getaway? Fancy her knowing something like that.'

'She knows everything,' said Les. 'Least, Mill thinks she does.'

'We ought to go over to Folletts' later, to see how Ned's doing. What d'you reckon?'

'If you like,' said Les and resumed his watch on the snow-covered clearing beyond the holly bush.

'I saw him when I was out there the other day,' said Frank. 'I was trying to borrow a ladder for Nan's roof. He's just a kid, Les. All he was doing was wandering about near his dad's farm and they shot him.'

'If you don't answer 'em when they challenge you that's what happens,' said Les.

'They do what they perishing-well like!' Frank stamped his foot. Though whether it was because he was angry or simply to get some feeling back into it was hard to tell. Then: 'Les?' he said.

'What?'

'Know what I was thinking about the other day?'

'What?'

'Me and you and Mr Sims dodging the Nasties that day in Seabourne, remember? And Mr Sims getting the bomb to Ted Naylor. Do you ever think about that?'

'Not much.'

'I do,' said Frank. 'Trouble is it's starting to feel like a story and not . . . well, not like something we actually did. It was all so secret. Still is. Nobody knows it was us. I don't mean I want them to think we were brave or clever or anything. What I mean is even Ted Naylor didn't know it was us who helped him, did he? But we can't have been the only ones. It doesn't make sense. If everybody who helped knew who they were it would make people feel strong . . . Don't you see what I mean?'

'The more people who know the more chance of the Nasties finding out,' said Les. 'They don't give up.'

'Well, then!'

'Well then, what?'

'If they don't give up then people haven't got anything to lose, have they? There's no point them giving up neither.'

Les shrugged.

'Come on, Les! What else is there to do?' said Frank in exasperation.

'We've just got to keep going,' said Les.

'And what about fighting back?'

'I don't know. I reckon Mr Thrale's got it about right.'

'How do you mean?'

'He just gets on with things. Looking after things. Keeping everything going.'

'Yes, but Les . . . ?' But Les didn't answer.

What was the matter with him? Frank had noticed that recently: Les had changed. Oh, it wasn't all the time, of course. But just occasionally. Like now. Les would suddenly turn cautious and sound like . . . well, sound just like now, just like Alec Thrale; and not at all like the mate who'd stuck by him and to whom Frank had stuck just as closely through thick and thin. That's how it had been ever since they'd arrived in the village. Always would be, wouldn't it? There was still nobody he relied on more. No one he'd rather have beside him in a jam. Not when George Poole and his gang started their stupid games; or when—if they ever got the chance again—it came to doing whatever had to be done to have another go at the Nasties. Still, there was no question about it, Les had changed. And Frank wondered if he'd changed too? It didn't feel like it but . . .

'Frank!' Les suddenly pulled Frank down beside him. 'By the tree,' he whispered.

The rabbit was moving cautiously towards the edge of the wood. A few more feet and it would pass into the snare. The boys held their breath and waited.

Then, when it was only another hop from the wire, there was a loud crash, like something falling. The rabbit's ears went up and it turned and bolted into the undergrowth.

Les was on his feet. 'It's them!' he yelled, grabbing the stick he'd brought with him. 'They're over there!'

They were there all right. And they weren't making any effort to conceal their presence. The boys crashed through the undergrowth until they found themselves at the edge of the wood.

The half-canvassed truck was parked in the middle of the road. In the back was a trestle-table with a wireless receiver standing on it. A long wire aerial swayed above it; and on the roof of the cab a metal ring was turning slowly. Hunched in front of the receiver was a young soldier. The driver sat in the cab smoking; and a sergeant and three other soldiers were leaning against the truck or standing nearby stamping their feet to keep warm. As the boys emerged from the wood one of them threw his rifle to his shoulder and snatched at the safety-catch. Les dropped the stick and they both threw their arms in the air.

The sergeant pulled the rifle down. '*Vorsicht,*' he said, '*Vorsicht!*' He walked towards where the boys were standing. '*Wollen Sie sich umbringen?*' he shouted angrily. '*Num geht schon! Schnell!* Go away from here! Now!'

Frank and Les stumbled down the bank and ran off along the road.

The sergeant watched them go then turned and looked back at his detail. He'd really pulled the short straw this time. Standing in the snow playing nursemaid to this 'expert' and his nonsense. 'Get a move on, Mainz!' he called. 'Stalingrad can't be much colder than this!'

But the young man on the lorry was engrossed in the map which he had open in front of him. With his own detecting ring and the information from the vehicles patrolling the other sides of the triangle all he needed was one more transmission. One broadcast was all he needed. Ah, but this fellow was sly. He transmitted only rarely and shifted his position each time. And now he seemed to have shut down completely. Dieter Mainz pulled off his headphones and looked apologetically at the sergeant. 'I would like to try further on, sergeant,' he said.

His companions cursed him and clambered back on board the lorry. The sergeant slammed the tailboard shut and they drove off up the road.

The poor man looked so cold standing there in the snow. But she really had quite enough brushes to be going on with.

'They're not an item that wears out with any great frequency,' she explained.

'It's not a matter of wear, madam, it's a question of

efficiency,' her caller replied, and blew on his fingers. 'The scientific redistribution of bristle has increased the cleaning power of even our least expensive lines by over thirty per cent. If I might be allowed to demonstrate for you . . . '

'Oh, very well. You'd better come in.'

'You won't regret it, madam.'

'Miss,' she said, 'Miss Elizabeth Firth.'

'Crompton—Stan Crompton,' he said, taking off his hat.

He followed her into the kitchen. And hoped she'd offer him a cup of tea. She looked the sort who would. And she did.

And with the tea—some horrible, fruit-flavoured brew—came the chat. As he'd known it would. Even while he was giving her the patter he could see she was just waiting for the opportunity. And an apparently casual enquiry he made about the age of the house provided it. That was all she needed and she was off nineteen-to-the-dozen.

Her father, Mr Denzil Firth, had bought it for himself and his new bride, she explained. That was at the turn of the century, of course. Sadly her dear mother had been carried off by the awful influenza epidemic which had claimed so many lives at the end of the Great War. She and her father had gone on living there. But ever afterwards, she said, the house had always felt strangely empty. She had lived there all her life. Apart from a brief period when she had gone away to London and worked for a firm of exporters. A firm in 'The City', she told him proudly; and, he thought, a little wistfully. But then she had had to return to Shevington, as was her duty, to nurse her father in the final years of his illness. Daddy had died not long before the outbreak of this present war. And now, except for her cat Gargery, she lived here quite alone.

Which wasn't the part of the story he'd actually wanted to hear. Still, he'd got her going and that was a start. 'But you've always been a very active member of the community, haven't you?' he said. 'Didn't someone tell me you were the Village Warden at one time? You know, when the military first arrived? That must have been a very responsible position.'

'It was,' she replied; 'very responsible. And very demanding.' Operating as intermediary between the German authorities and the villagers, Betty Firth recalled only too well, had been a misunderstood and thankless task. Keeping an eye on things, maintaining records, filling in forms, writing reports: her work had been a source of constant friction. But it was a task which she had carried out faithfully, despite the brickbats and petty hostilities she had encountered on all sides. 'I was attempting to help things back to normal as quickly as possible,' she told him. 'I felt it was my duty, at the time.'

'But not any more?'

'There were certain excesses which occurred, Mr Crompton.'

'You mean the reprisals at Middelbury?'

'Quite so.'

'Quite so.' Crompton took another mouthful of the tea. 'Odd business, all round,' he said. 'The attack on Shevington Hall, I mean.'

'Odd, Mr Crompton?'

'To be honest, a number of folk, people I've spoken to, have told me what happened that night and . . . ' Stan Crompton shook his head. 'But . . . No! It makes no sense at all!'

'What makes no sense?'

'I'm damned if . . . oh, do pardon my French . . . what I mean is I can't believe for the life of me there was just the one man, this Ted Naylor chap, involved in a thing like that.'

Betty Firth's cornflower blue eyes flashed. 'He would not have wanted for assistance, Mr Crompton,' she said. 'Not in Shevington.'

'Is that a fact? No, thank you.' Crompton placed a hand over his cup as she tilted the teapot in his direction. 'Of course, as one-time Warden, Miss Firth, you must know just about everything there is to know about people round here. Would I be correct in assuming that you harbour, shall we say, suspicions on the matter?'

'You would be quite correct. As you may know, Mr Crompton, Naylor took the names of his associates to the grave. But I've always thought . . . It's only a suspicion, of course . . . but I've always thought that woman Tate must have been involved in some way.'

'Really?'

'Oh, yes! She was a constant thorn. Always playing the Bolshie! Flouting authority, mine and everyone else's. And flitting about on that bicycle of hers. That woman . . . Oh, dear, I've gone much too far. It really isn't my place to suggest such a thing to a stranger.'

'I say!' exclaimed Crompton indignantly. 'Do I look like the sort of man who can't be trusted with confidences of that nature?'

'No, of course not,' she said quickly. 'I didn't mean to impugn your discretion, Mr Crompton.'

'Miss Firth, in times such as these discretion is one of the few things an honest man has left to cling to.'

Mr Crompton's eloquence was unexpected. Indeed, he displayed several qualities that surprised Betty Firth. For one, he didn't persist in trying to sell her any of those awful brushes. And then . . .

'And did you pass on your suspicions to the authorities?' he enquired.

'Certainly not. They were suspicions, Mr Crompton, and no more than that. I always strove to fill my reports with facts; I always tried to avoid tittle-tattle and rumour. Difficult as that was.'

'How admirable. If only there were more like you, dear lady. But I mustn't monopolize any more of your time. Duty calls. And I daresay you've lots to be getting on with.' Crompton replaced his cup and saucer on the table and got up. 'It has been a great pleasure meeting you, Miss Firth; and spending time, however briefly, in your charming home. And that was the best cup of tea I've had for many a long month. Good afternoon.'

Such a polite and unpredictable little man, she thought, as she watched him walk down the path with his case of samples. How deceptive appearances could be.

Vera Thrale was always full of surprises. The first time Mill ever saw her it was Vera herself who had been the surprise. She had appeared in the doorway of the Thrales' cottage wearing a threadbare silk dressing-gown with what looked like a man's tie knotted round it. And she'd been wearing one of Alec's caps.

Mill and Les and the battered pram containing all they possessed had gone right through Shevington and were almost out the other side when they stopped at the Thrales' to ask for a drink of water. With hardly a second glance Vera had invited them in. And there they had remained. Mill was supposed to earn their keep by helping with the housework but she'd never felt like a servant because Vera had never treated her like one.

Vera was . . . ? Well, Vera was Vera. And quite unlike anyone Mill had ever met before. You'd have taken her for a toff, and, of course, she was; but she didn't behave like one. Oh, she had her funny ways, and half the time you couldn't understand what she was talking about—mind you, she was very clever, there was no question of that—but she always treated you like someone who was just the same as she was. And, yes, she was always full of surprises.

Like this afternoon. Though this time it hadn't been a surprise Mill enjoyed very much. Despite her protestations she had been taken along the passage to Vera's room and made to sit down opposite her modelling board.

'I'm going to start your head, Mildred,' Vera had announced.

It was something she'd been meaning to do for some time. The ungainly, plain girl who had come to the door that day two years ago had changed. It wasn't an ugly-duckling-into-swan sort of change, Vera decided; it was subtler than that. Mildred was beginning . . . to be herself. And it made her beautiful. And it needed recording. That and a certain happy glow she seemed to have acquired recently. If the clay could only capture that too.

'It won't take long,' she assured her model. 'Just try to keep reasonably still, dear.'

But keeping still—even reasonably still—was difficult when you felt so uncomfortable. And even though she wanted to please Vera, Mill found it almost impossible to bear.

After a while Vera stopped. 'Is this agony for you?' she said.

Mill nodded. And added apologetically: 'I don't like people looking at me, Mrs Thrale. I can't help it.'

'But you have a strong, beautiful face. And your colouring . . . ' Vera threw the wet cloth over the clay and wiped her hands on her apron. 'I know just the thing that would set off your colouring! Why didn't I think of it before?' She crossed the room and knelt down in front of the empty fireplace. 'Open, Sesame!' she intoned theatrically. Then she reached up and began to run her hand over the bricks.

'What are you doing, Mrs Thrale?'

'It's a secret.'

'Sorry,' said Mill and turned away.

'Don't be silly. It's not a secret from you. I trust you implicitly, dear.' Vera removed two bricks and placed them next to her on the floor. 'It was an old bread oven,' she explained. 'Someone blocked it in, years and years ago.' She reached in and lifted out a narrow, rectangular box covered in worn, green velvet. She opened it and held it out for Mill to see. Inside was a necklace of dark red stones.

Vera smiled. 'Rubies. Aren't they pretty? All my worldly wealth! My mother slipped them to me after father cut me off without a penny. After I told them I was going to marry Alec.'

'Mrs Thrale! That's just like in a book,' said Mill.

'A rather sad and silly book, dear. My father was so angry. You know my parents and one or two of their circle sold up in London and bought a farm not far from here? This was long before the war. It was an experiment. I'm afraid the community broke up after a year or two and they all drifted back to Hampstead. But I stayed. With Alec. And my dear mother gave me these so that I wouldn't starve.' Vera laughed. 'Who knows—perhaps they may save us all from a similar fate. Now . . . ' She slipped the necklace around Mill's neck and fastened it. Then she reached for a hand-mirror. 'There,' she said. 'Look at yourself!'

'Nah,' said Mill her face flushed with embarrassment.

'I wish you would.'

But Mill had turned her head away.

Vera smiled and put down the mirror. 'Another day, perhaps.'

Mill watched her replace the jewel-box in its hiding-place. She wished she hadn't shown her. It was nice to be trusted. But the trouble was she wasn't sure she ought to be trusted. He'd been there again the next day. And the day after that. All they did was chat and walk along, that was all. Not where anybody could see or anything, of course. So there wasn't any harm in it. It was nice. And what was really nice was the way he always called her . . . Vera would know about that, wouldn't she? Vera knew everything.

'Mrs Thrale?'

'Yes, dear?'

'Mrs Thrale, what sort of a name is Millicent?'

'Millicent?'

'Yes.'

'Whatever made you think of that?'

'Nuffin',' said Mill quickly. 'I think I read it somewhere, that's all.'

'I believe the name Millicent is originally Teutonic. German. It means "strong and true".' Vera smiled. 'It would be a particularly good name for you, dear. Because that's what you are. Of course, Mildred's a lovely name, too.'

'I s'pose so,' said Mill. But Millicent, she thought, was nicer.

When Frank and Les arrived at Nan's in search of a warm they found that Nan already had a visitor. He had drawn his chair close to hers and stretched his wet shoes towards the fire.

'This is Mr Crompton,' she said. 'He's trying to sell me a brush. This is Frank and Les, Mr Crompton. Frank's my grandson.'

'Stan's the name,' said Crompton smiling. 'We've met before. You're the young chap who told me the way, aren't you?'

Frank nodded. The more he saw of Mr Stanley Crompton the less he liked.

'What have you two been up to?' said Nan.

'Trying to catch the toe-rags who've been nicking our snares,' said Les.

'And did you?'

'Nah. There were some Jerries up in the woods. I reckon they probably scared them off.'

'What were the Jerries doing in the woods?'

'They had a wireless or something on the back of a lorry,' said Frank.

'Whatever for?'

'We didn't 'xactly wait to find out.'

'Very wise. Discretion being the better part of valour, eh?' said Crompton, getting to his feet. 'Well, needs must! I'm off to cast my bread on other waters.' He closed his samples case and tucked it under his arm. 'And thank you for your time, Mrs Tate. I've enjoyed our chat. And I hope I may not be unwelcome on another occasion?'

'I always enjoy a chat.'

'And there's no obligation, of course—none whatsoever. Mind you, I never give up.'

'Like Garibaldi,' she said.

'Garibaldi?' He grinned. 'Quite so. Though I believe he was a rather taller cove than I am. Well, all the best, boys.'

'Shifty perisher,' said Frank when Crompton had gone. 'You're not going to buy any of his brushes, are you?'

''Course not,' said Nan.

They sat by the fire and chatted for half an hour or more. But then it was obvious Nan was tired and Frank gave Les the nod and he got up to go.

'I've got to get back, Mrs Tate,' he said. 'I help Mr Thrale with collecting firewood last thing.'

'You're a good boy, Les. No,' she said, 'no, you're not boys no more, neither of you. You're men nigh on.' She sighed. 'Ah, but you've had to grow up fast. Too fast. Will you promise me something? Both of you?'

They nodded.

'You're to look out for each other. Yes, I know that you do but . . . just don't forget to always look out for each other, all right? Promise me you'll do that whatever happens.'

''Course, Mrs Tate.'

''Course,' said Frank. 'See you later, Nan.'

Colin Worth watched his cousin and his friend leave. And saw Nan settle herself into her chair.

'Nan?' he said.

She looked round in surprise and found him in the doorway. 'Colin? Have you been standing there listening?' she said.

'I was in the hall. I couldn't help it, Nan,' he said. 'Nan, am I a good boy as well?'

'Whatever makes you ask?'

He shrugged. 'Am I, Nan?'

'Yes, Colin,' she said, 'you're a good boy, too.'

'Then why . . . ' he hesitated. 'Then why don't our dad talk to me?'

Nan looked up at his troubled face and shook her head. 'Listen, that en't no fault of yours, Colin. You mustn't think that.'

'But why doesn't he come down and sit with the rest of us? And tell us things. I was looking forward to that.'

'Have you tried telling *him* things? How about telling him all the things you said you'd saved up to tell him?'

'He won't listen.'

'Don't mean you shouldn't keep trying. You find something to tell him that'll really interest him, eh? Will you do that, Colin?'

'All right, Nan.'

'Good boy.'

Colin watched her turn back to the fire. That was easy enough to say, he thought; but Nan didn't know what it was like. She didn't know what his father was like. Sitting up in that room all day, staring out of the window, and never even looking at you when you spoke to him. Like you wasn't there at all. Like he wasn't there at all.

'Here, Frank—what did your gran say all that for?' said Les, as they walked down the path towards the wash-house. 'All that about looking out for each other? I mean, we do, don't we—look out for each other?'

'Far as I know,' said Frank. 'Always have done.'

'She's all right, your gran. Pity she can't get about so much any more.'

'She never recovered after that Jerry lorry ran her into the ditch.'

'She used to be out all the time on that bike,' said Les. 'How's it doing?'

Frank lifted the tarpaulin. 'Rusting up. See, on the handlebars?'

'It's not in bad nick, though. A drop of oil on them

wheels and she'd be right as rain. Blimey, Frank—just think if you had a bike! Ain't you never asked her?'

Frank shook his head. 'I can't do that.'

'Why not?'

Frank shrugged. He'd wanted to ask her. He'd wanted to ask Nan about the bike so many times! Oh, it was a woman's bike, of course, but that didn't matter. A bike of any sort meant you could come and go as you pleased. With a bike you could be as free as a bird. But he could never bring himself to ask. Because he knew that for her to part with her bicycle would be an admission of something much too painful. It would be too much even for Nan. Even for Nan who would have given him anything in the world. Because it was Nan who had once been as free as a bird.

'It's hers, Les,' he said. 'I can't ask her that.'

He replaced the tarpaulin; and looked up and saw the figure watching them from the upstairs window. Len Worth was wearing his old overcoat and his shoulders were hunched against the cold; or against some blow he always seemed to be waiting to fall.

'Does he sit up there all day?' asked Les.

Frank nodded.

'What's he think about?'

'Search me.'

Chapter 5

Peter Sims watched as the elderly man and the labrador dog came slowly across The Green and stopped outside the school gates.

Mr Underwood had been headmaster at Shevington School for as long as most of the village could remember. He'd taught the parents of the children who were pupils there now. With his dignified, old-fashioned bearing he was a reminder to them all of a time when everything had always seemed to be in order, a time when things were always where you'd left them.

'Good morning, Mr Underwood.'

'Good morning, Mr Sims. Have you had to close up again?'

'I've badgered them till I'm blue in the face but there is still no sign of any coal.'

'These must be very trying times for you. But, tell me, otherwise? You are coping?'

Sims ran his fingers through his hair. And sighed: 'Not as well as you used to, Mr Underwood.'

'Come, come, Mr Sims, I have every confidence in you.'

'You're very kind.'

'And yourself? Are you finding a little time for yourself? I know how difficult that can be. The monograph, now—how is that progressing?'

'The monograph?' said Sims. 'Yes, I'm . . . I'm getting on.'

'Good. My wife and I take great comfort from your efforts, you know. It is an enormous consolation to know that Henry's work will come to fruition after all. Take all the time you need.' Mr Underwood smiled. 'Though, of course, we look forward immensely to reading your conclusions. Well, I must push on. And don't worry, you'll cope; I am quite certain you will. Come along, Bess!'

The old labrador stumbled to her feet and waddled away at the heels of her master.

Peter Sims walked back to his office. He couldn't help feeling Mr Underwood's confidence was misplaced. Cope? When he couldn't even organize a bag of coal to heat the classrooms? When his pupils were shot and he could do nothing about it?

And as for the Patfield monograph to which Mr Underwood and his wife were so looking forward . . . Getting on? Wasn't that what he'd said? Oh dear, that was an even worse source of guilt. The monograph could have been finished months ago! Of course it could. Though the fact that it wasn't certainly wasn't due to any negligence or sloth on his part. He worked on it during every spare waking moment. Sometimes he would even get up during the night to reconsider some piece of evidence, connect an argument, or refine a conclusion. Those ruins filled his life. He knew why, of course. He knew that the distant past was a refuge for him, a familiar country which he could travel without maps, where he even spoke the language. He knew the truth was that once he was there he didn't want to leave. Because it was the safest place to be. Inevitably, when the real world and its future was so uncertain; or, at best, so unpalatable. Oh, he knew all that. He knew he was constantly trying to delay the day when he would have to hand the manuscript back to the Underwoods. Like Penelope, he thought, like the wife of Odysseus unravelling her tapestry each night so that it would never be complete and she wouldn't have to give her suitors an answer. Oh, dear . . .

He looked up in answer to the knock at his door. 'Come in,' he called. 'Tate?'

'I was just passing, sir.'

Frank stood half in and half out of the room and neither of them spoke. Until:

'Is something wrong?' said Sims.

'No,' said Frank.

'I'm sorry, Tate, but there are one or two things I've got to . . . '

'Me and Les were talking the other afternoon, sir . . . about the old days.'

'The old days?'

'Yes. You know. The time . . . that day we brought the bomb back from Seabourne.'

Sims got quickly to his feet. 'Good heavens, Tate, what are you thinking of! Close the door at once!'

'Sorry, sir.'

'The authorities have spies everywhere, you know that. They are always listening. You really should take more care.'

'We were just remembering, that's all.'

'That all seems a long time ago, Tate.'

'Was it a waste of time, sir? Nothing came of it. Not in the end.'

'They say there is still resistance. In the far north. And in Wales. And these rumours of the American landings in Morocco give one cause for optimism.'

'But it's not the same.'

'The same, Tate? No; no, it isn't.' No, it wasn't the same, thought Sims ruefully. The whole affair with the bomb had been very frightening at the time; but, dear heavens, he still remembered how proud he had felt when it was over! Because he had been quite brave. No, that was putting it rather too strongly. After all, for some of the time he hadn't even known that it was a bomb in the basket they'd collected from Seabourne that day. Even so, despite everything, it would be fair to say—he had behaved well.

'Knowing someone else is fighting isn't the same as having a go at them yourself,' said Frank. 'But nobody does.'

'When you recall what von Schreier and his myrmidons did to Middelbury, Tate, you can understand why people think twice before opposing them.'

'They shouldn't. Think twice, I mean.'

'People have a lot to lose.'

'But that's just it, sir—they haven't! Not any more. That's what I told Les.'

'I confess, I envy you your single-mindedness,' said the teacher. 'But, look here, you must be careful what you say, you know. The people at the Hall would dearly love to get their hands on anyone who was involved in our . . . our adventure. Their spies are everywhere.'

'You mean like that chap who lodges with you?' said Frank.

Sims frowned. 'Mr Crompton? Whyever do you say that?'

Frank shrugged. 'I keep seeing him everywhere, that's all,' he said. And added, 'I mean, he'd be the sort they'd use to sniff something out, wouldn't he?'

'Come now . . . '

'Nobody knows anything about him, do they? And . . . '

'Good Lord, Tate, we can't suspect someone just because they're a stranger. Miss Meacher?'

Miss Meacher hesitated in the doorway. 'I'm so sorry, Mr Sims,' she said, 'I didn't realize there was someone with you. I would have knocked.'

'It's quite all right. Tate just looked in to see if he could help in any way. Thank you, Tate. Perhaps tomorrow, eh?'

'Right you are, sir.'

'Such an obliging boy,' she said when Frank had gone.

'Indeed,' Sims replied. And looked hard at the young woman opposite. Had Audrey Meacher been listening at the door? Had she? And if she had, for how long had she been standing there? Was it possible *she* might be . . . ?

'Is something wrong, Mr Sims?'

'Wrong, Miss Meacher?' Good Lord, what was

happening to him? What was he thinking of? 'No, nothing—nothing at all,' he said.

'I've brought you a flask of tea.'

'That's very kind.'

She watched him unscrew the cup from the top of the flask. 'You seem a little perkier, Mr Sims,' she ventured, 'if I may say so. Is your fellow guest proving less intrusive?'

'Crompton? Oh, yes. Yes, he keeps himself much more to himself. Exhausted, I imagine. He seems to be very busy. I hear him come and go at all hours. It's all perfectly normal.'

'I'm relieved to hear it,' she said.

But the look she gave him seemed to say: Oh, dear. You think that's perfectly normal, do you?

'I do hope you're right,' she said. 'These people can be so extraordinarily devious. One must always be on one's guard—don't you think?'

He had to go past them. There was no way to avoid it. Besides, he wouldn't have walked round them even if he could. That wasn't Frank's way.

When he reached the other side of The Green the group of boys standing outside The Shevington Arms turned to look at him. Though they'd known he was coming ever since he'd left the school gates.

The landlord's son, George Poole, grinned. 'Here he is, then!' he said. 'Frank Tate! Here's the only one who won't never go 'ungry.'

'Why's that, George?' several voices demanded eagerly.

'Stands to reason, don't it? 'Course he won't. Cos . . . cos . . . ' George Poole was already doubled up at his own joke. 'Cos he's a Tater, ain't he? So he could allus eat hisself!'

The others laughed.

It was always the way. It had been since Frank first arrived in the village. It was how Poole and his pals liked it. George especially. George Poole had made himself boss and the rest of them were too frightened to cross him. He was bigger than they were. Louder and mouthier too.

It was Les they'd picked on first. Les Gill had been their first stranger. They'd tormented him in the playground, the classroom, anywhere they could corner him. 'Gyppo' they'd called him; because he was small and dark. And then, when Frank arrived and took his side, they'd turned on Frank. Besides, Frank was an outsider too, wasn't he? And two targets were twice the fun. That's how it had gone on. To begin with. But together, as time passed, Frank and Les had seen them off. And now Poole's gang thought twice about picking on either of them. Though Poole himself still couldn't resist the opportunity.

'Know what we ought to call him, George?' said Wally Carr, the policeman's son. '"King Edward", that's what we ought to call him. That's a sort of tater, ennit?'

'So's "Mary Piper",' said Poole. ''Ow you doin', Mary?'

They all laughed again. But they made sure they kept their distance. Frank had a temper most of them had painful reasons to remember at one time or another.

'And d'you know what I likes alongside a tater?' said Poole. 'I don't reckon you can beat a nice fresh bit of rabbit! What about you, Tater? Like a bit of bunny in the pot, do you? You and the gyppo?'

Frank turned back and walked over to him. The others quickly stood aside. 'I know it's you, Poole,' he said.

'Me what?'

'I know it's you who's stealing from our snares.'

'Now you hold on,' Poole replied. 'Tha's slander, that is. Don't you go accusin' me like that, Frank Tate!' He smiled. 'Cos you got no proof. You better take that back or our dad'll come and sort you out.'

Frank looked down at the other boy's boots. They were big. Almost a man's. But were they big enough?

'One of these days, George,' he said. 'One of these days you're going to get paid back good and proper!'

'That'll be nice,' replied Poole. But he made sure he waited until Frank had walked away.

'I find the countryside is not a cheerful place, Millicent.'

'How d'you mean?'

'It is so quiet. Like you I am from the city. I miss the noises and the crowded streets.'

'I don't,' said Mill. 'I used to. But not no more.'

They were walking along the road some way beyond the village. It was where they'd walked last time. And the time before that. It was where they were least likely to meet anyone. Though nowhere was really safe. But once they were walking together and talking it didn't seem so bad. He was so easy to talk to that you forgot all the . . . well, all the rest of it.

'You could probably get to like it,' she said, 'if you was here long enough.' When he didn't reply she asked tentatively: 'Do you think you will be?'

'I am a soldier,' he said. 'I have to go where I am sent. Our armies are in many places. From Stalingrad to Paris. Who knows where they will be next.'

'I s'pose so.' They walked on. 'But it ain't always going to be like this, is it?' she said. 'I mean, one day it's bound to be over.'

'Of course.'

They made an odd couple. The big, dark-haired girl and the slight, fair young man; walking along with their hands plunged deep into the pockets of their coats, and always keeping a foot or more distance between them.

'D'you think a lot about where you come from?' she asked.

'At first I missed Dresden very much,' he said. 'But not so much now. I think of it less now. It is . . . ' He searched for the word. 'Helpful. It is helpful to have someone to talk to.'

'Who?'

'You, of course.'

'Me?'

'You are my good friend, Millicent.' He saw her shake her head. 'Yes, you are. But I wonder why you tell me so little about yourself.'

'Nuffin' to tell,' she said.

'I don't even know where you live.'

'You're the interestin' one. And you still ain't told me what it is you do exactly.'

'My work . . . '

The sound of a vehicle approaching turned his head. And he stepped back quickly into the shelter of the hedge. The van went by and disappeared around the bend. When it was gone he stepped out again.

'We are safe now,' he said.

'What d'you do that for?' she said.

'I am aware what people will say if they see you with me. You do not deserve such a thing. I would not like us to be unable to walk out together.'

'We're not walking out together,' she said quickly.

'I think we are.'

She felt herself blushing. 'Are we? It's just that . . . it means something different here, that's all,' she said, 'walking out with someone.'

'Oh?' he said.

They walked on for a while in silence. Then: 'What was you going to say?' she asked. 'Before that car come by? You know, about your work?'

'It is difficult to tell you, Millicent.'

'You don't do something bad, do you, Dieter? You ain't the Gestapo or nothing?'

'No!' He laid a hand on her sleeve. 'No, Millicent. You must not think such a thing. I told you, I am . . . I am a wireless operator.'

'Is that an important job?'

'For me? Yes! Before I was called into the army I had no trade or skill to find work with. My future was very bleak. Now, when the war is over, I will be able to . . . I would like to open a shop, perhaps.'

'What sort of shop?'

'To sell radios. All sorts of radios. Best of all to make them, perhaps.'

'Is that what your work is, then? Making radios?'

'My work . . . Millicent, I cannot tell you what my work is.'

'What, cos I'm the enemy?'

'You are not my enemy,' he said. And she noticed that his hand had remained on her sleeve. 'You are my friend.'

'Am I?' she said.

'Millicent, I hope that I am your friend?'

'I s'pose.' Mill shrugged and hunched her hot face inside the collar of her coat.

'I am glad,' he said. 'We should walk on.'

'Dieter,' she said, 'if you had a shop . . . '

Colin Worth looked round the door. His father was sitting where he always sat in front of the window looking down on the back garden. He knocked cautiously but Len didn't respond.

'Dad?' he said. But there was no answer. 'Dad, I've found it.'

'Found what?'

Colin hurried across the room and offered his father the book. It was his precious encyclopaedia. The book that always lay next to his bed. Whenever anything was in doubt, a place, a name, a fact, Colin would reach for it and consult its pages. There was no question the encyclopaedia couldn't answer or problem it couldn't solve.

'I've found Morocco,' he said.

'Is that a fact?'

'There's a picture of some Arabs. They've got rifles and they're riding camels. And there's a map. But there's loads of it and I don't know where to look. Dad, where do you think the Americans have landed?'

'Who says they have?'

'Everybody.'

'And you always believe what everybody says, do you?'

'Only if . . .'

'It's a rumour, Colin; that's all it is.'

'But, Dad, news like that has got to come from somewhere.'

'Out of people's heads. That's where it comes from.'

'Yes, but—'

'No buts, Colin. There's no buts about it. It's just what people want to believe, that's all. It's the sort of tale people tell themselves. Whistling in the dark, it's called. That's all there is to it. That's all there is to any of it.'

'But, Dad, they're fighting the Japanese. The Americans are on our side.'

'For God's sake, boy!' Len Worth turned from the window. 'It's not the pictures! Nobody's going to come riding over the hill blowing trumpets. Nobody's coming to the rescue. It's not like that. It ain't a bit like that. You take it from me. You take it from one who knows.'

Colin stared at him open-mouthed. There were tears in his father's eyes.

'Len?' Edie had appeared at the door. 'Len?' she said. 'Whatever is it?'

'Nothing,' he said. 'Just leave me alone, both of you. Just leave me be. That's not too much to ask, is it?'

'Come on, Colin,' she said. 'Come downstairs and give your dad some peace and quiet.'

Agnes Elliott added more hot water to the used tea leaves. She sighed as she replaced the lid on the pot. How long it seemed since it had contained their own careful blend of lapsang souchong and best Assam: An eternity!

'And because there is so little petrol available he now

walks everywhere,' said her sister. 'Even in this dreadful weather.'

'And yet he is always so cheerful!' said Agnes. 'Everyone you meet has only a good word to say of him. Don't you find that, Mr Sims?'

'Find what, Miss Elliott? Do forgive me, my mind was elsewhere.'

'We were talking of dear Mr Crompton,' said Miss Florence.

'Ah, yes.' It seemed everyone was talking of 'dear Mr Crompton'. And after his exchange with young Tate and with Miss Meacher that morning Peter Sims had been thinking of him most of the day. And the teacher had come to a decision regarding what he must do about his garrulous fellow guest. He'd intended doing it the moment he returned that evening. But his landladies and Ilkley had intercepted him as he arrived in the hall. It had been impossible to decline the invitation to share their meal. Little enough as there was to share. Yet the doilies were still set out on the cake-stand and the damask napkins still rolled in their ivory napkin rings. And the watery brew was served from the Sèvres service with all the occasion of high-tea at Fortnum and Mason's. They actually bothered. And probably always would. Keeping up appearances was so important to them. He wanted to find their absurd gentility reassuring. But what did it mean in a world where the secret policeman and the bully-boy were so vigorously triumphant?

'He is a lesson to us all,' said Miss Agnes. 'And so amusing.'

'"There's always dust!" Isn't that what he says, Agnes?' said Miss Florence. 'Ilkley! Naughty creature!' The terrier had taken Sims's trouser turn-up and was tugging at it playfully. 'Oh, do forgive him, Mr Sims.'

Sims stood up, grateful for the excuse. 'Please don't trouble yourselves,' he said. 'Thank you very much indeed for the tea. It was, as always, most enjoyable. But I really must get on.'

'We see so little of you these days,' said Miss Agnes. 'And you know you are always welcome.'

'Thank you.'

'You are still our favourite,' said Miss Florence coyly.

Ilkley bounced after him barking and running circles round his feet until Mr Sims was able finally to slip around the door and make his escape.

'Isn't it odd,' said Miss Agnes, 'how Ilkley carries on so. You'd think he would be used to Mr Sims after all this time.'

'Yes,' said her sister. 'And he never makes a sound when Mr Crompton comes and goes.'

'Mr Crompton is such a quiet gentleman.'

Peter Sims hurried upstairs to his room. He switched on the light, then stepped out again and closed the door loudly.

He listened for a moment. Then he tiptoed along the landing. When he reached Crompton's door he paused. There was no tell-tale light beneath it. He reached for the handle, turned it slowly, and stepped inside.

The curtains were open and there was just enough light to see by. Unlike his own rooms Crompton's was a simple bed-sitting room; it was a small, high-ceilinged room with a bay-window giving on to the garden at the back of the house.

Where to begin? What was he looking for? Something, anything, to give some indication of . . . Of what? Oh, dear, he really should have planned this more carefully. Some indication of . . . A sign that Crompton was not what he appeared to be! Yes! That was it. And what sort of sign might that be? Well, he was sure he would recognize it when he saw it.

Crompton was obviously a tidy man. Excessively so. There were few signs that the room was occupied. The bed had been carefully made. And on the table beside it was a lamp and beside the lamp a book, *The Sidewinder*, with a gaudy cover depicting a stetsonned cowboy levelling a smoking six-gun at a moustachioed figure standing outside a western saloon. That, Sims thought, would inevitably be Crompton's taste in literature. Next to the book was a bottle of pills labelled 'painkillers', a dusty carafe of water, and a glass. In what was otherwise such an anonymous room the pills seemed a touchingly personal item. And for the first time Sims felt like an intruder. He stopped and looked over his shoulder guiltily. There was a suitcase on top of the wardrobe but he decided he would leave that for the moment. Instead, he opened the wardrobe door; and was greeted by the smell of lavender and moth balls. There was nothing hanging inside or folded on the shelves. Mr Crompton obviously travelled light. And today he was travelling even lighter. Because there was his samples case.

Sims was reaching down to pick it up when something made him turn.

Stan Crompton was standing in the doorway. He had one hand deep in the pocket of his overcoat and the other gripped the handle of his samples case.

'Was it a brush you were looking for, old man?' he said.

Chapter 6

Crompton closed the door quietly.

And Sims stepped away from the wardrobe. 'Look here, Crompton,' he said, 'this isn't what it appears to be.'

'Is that a fact?' said the salesman. 'No, please stay where you are. We're neither of us the physical type, are we? And coming to blows isn't going to accomplish anything. Besides, I wouldn't want to distress the dear ladies.' He placed his case on the counterpane and switched on the bedside lamp. 'Now then,' he said, 'I think it's time you and I had a serious chinwag, don't you?'

'What do you want?'

'Shouldn't I be asking that, old man? Well, time is short, I suppose.' Crompton sat down on the bed. 'Where shall we start? All right—not to beat about the bush, you're the chap who delivered the bomb that went off at the Hall two years ago, aren't you?'

'Good God!' Sims steadied himself against the wardrobe.

'I think you'd better take a pew, old man; there's more to come.'

Sims sat down abruptly on the end of the bed. 'Are you . . . are you the Gestapo?'

'Steady on,' said the salesman. And laughed. 'No, Mr Sims, I'm not the Gestapo.'

'But how do you know,' said Sims desperately, 'about the explosive device?'

'Ted Naylor's bomb? You're going to have to trust me on that one. Though I can understand that you'll require some kind of bona fides.' Crompton stood up and drew the curtains. Then he opened the lid of the samples case which he'd placed on the counterpane and lifted out the tray on which the brushes were displayed. Instead of a second layer of brushes what lay underneath was a neat array of dials, a length of wire, some headphones, and, in a narrow compartment to one side, a Morse-code key.

'There,' he said.

'Good Lord! Is it—What is it, a wireless?'

'That's right.'

'But the other case . . . the one in the wardrobe.'

'That one's full of brushes. That's the one I use door to door. The Nasties have even stopped me and looked inside that one.' Crompton grinned. 'Not the cheeriest five minutes of my life. Though it would have been a bit of a coup to sell them a Dust-Well Full Domestic, wouldn't it?'

'What are you doing with a wireless?'

'I have to deliver it, Mr Sims—rather urgently. There are people who need it and I've got to get it to them.'

'I see.'

'I need help, Mr Sims; I need your help.'

'My help? But I'm . . . '

'You've worked for the Resistance.'

'I'd hardly call what I did . . . '

'Don't do yourself down, Mr Sims. You got that bomb to Ted Naylor. That's the sort of help I need. And the help of your helpers. You had some, I imagine?'

'Good Lord, Crompton, I can't divulge . . . No, I don't think I can tell you something like that.'

'I thoroughly approve of your caution, old man, but I'm afraid you're going to have to.'

'But how . . . how do I know what you're saying is true? I don't even know if that really is a wireless you have there.'

'It's too perishin' heavy to be a joke, Mr Sims. Still, you're right to be cautious. Do you want me to tell you the address of the house where you collected the bomb?

Or I could tell you the names of some of the chaps who were at Cambridge with you—the "rather secret" society that sent you to Seabourne that day. I could tell you lots of things. But they'd be things the Gestapo could know just as well as our lot could. I suppose, in the end, your only reliable proof will be the fact that the Jerries don't come hammering on that door and cart you off the moment you've told me what you know. But time is pressing, Mr Sims. What do you say?'

Nan seemed to get up later and later these days. And once the boys had had their breakfast Edie had the kitchen to herself. Which was the way she liked it.

But this morning, for some reason, Rose was up earlier than usual. She sat with her cup of tea while her mother started the washing-up.

'Ma?' she said.

'What's that, Rose?'

'Ma, he doesn't ever mention going back to Swindon, does he?'

'Who, your father? No. Besides, there's not a lot of Swindon to go back to, is there? You know what Mrs Ward wrote us.'

'That's all right, then.'

'Rose! What an awful thing to say.'

'Eh? Oh, no! No, ma, I didn't mean it was all right what the Jerry bombers done. I just meant . . . well, it means we can stay here, doesn't it? I mean, I've got my job here and . . . ' Was this the time to tell her? She hesitated. But her mother didn't seem to notice. 'What I mean is I've got friends like Joycie Prout and Ivy Follett. I couldn't bear to leave them . . . and everything.'

'It's different for you, Rose. Swindon was where your father was born and brought up. It was his home. And the railway was his life.'

'What does he say about the house being bombed?'

Edie shrugged.

'He must say something, ma. Ma?'

Edie looked away. 'There's nothing he can say, Rose. Because he doesn't know.'

'Ma!'

'Oh, Rose, I can't bring meself to tell him. I couldn't bring meself to tell him when I used to write to him in that camp and I can't now. You can see the state he's in.'

'But, ma . . . '

'He's not the man that went away to fight any more. You remember him then, Rose; you remember what he was like. Oh, I know it wasn't easy—it wasn't easy for anybody before the war—but we had a proper life together, didn't we? Do you remember the four of us going out to the pictures? And how he used to take you children to the park of a Sunday morning? And he was in line for promotion, you know. Yes. There was a chargehand's job he'd been promised in the Repair Sheds. That would have been his for life, Rose. Things would have got . . . '

'What is it?'

'That's what he used to say: "Things'll be better, Edie. For the four of us." And I know it hurts him to know those dreams have come to nothing. Never mind all the rest of what's happened to him. Sometimes, Rose . . . '

'What?'

'Sometimes I wonder if we should have left.'

'What? Stayed and got bombed? Don't be daft, ma; you were right to bring us here.'

'He's not at home here, Rose. It's like he's lost. Try and talk to him more, eh? He always thought the world of you, you know.'

'I have tried, ma. But he hardly says a word to me. It's horrible. And when he does say anything to anybody it's grumpy or downright nasty.'

'It's because he's unhappy, Rose.'

'I'm not surprised. Sitting up at that window all day. He might just as well have stayed in the prison camp.'

'Rose! Don't you ever let him—' As Edie turned to pick up the dishcloth she caught sight of Len standing in the doorway.

'Len!' she exclaimed. 'Len, we didn't hear you come down. We didn't know you were—'

'No,' he said, pulling his overcoat round him, 'I gathered that.'

And he turned and went back upstairs.

'Dad?' called Rose. She got up to follow him but her mother held her by the arm.

'Best leave it,' she said. 'The damage is done now.'

Vera knew.

Mill was sure she knew because she had been looking at her funny. Yes, Vera knew something was going on. Well, not 'going on'. Because there wasn't anything 'going on'. Just meeting him and talking and walking along together wasn't 'going on'.

Vera knew. But Mill couldn't imagine how. 'Course, she had been going out every day round about the same time. That couldn't be helped because it was the only time Dieter could get away.

So this morning she had left much much earlier. It meant she had to wait about in the cold for him but she didn't mind that.

And as she waited she wondered: I mean, what if Vera did suspect something? It didn't matter, did it? After all, Vera understood things like that. Like what? Well, a thing like the fact that you couldn't help liking Dieter. Because . . . Oh, he was so polite! And he listened to what you said to him. And he told you things. Like about opening that shop. That was so nice. And as for the rest? It didn't do to think about the rest, about what might happen; nobody thought about that any more because nobody seemed to know what might happen any more. Your wildest dreams could come true and what you feared most in the world could come just as true. So Mill had begun to let herself dream. Vera would understand that, wouldn't she?

The sound of a motorcycle made her look back towards the village. As the machine came into sight the engine cut out and it slithered to a halt almost tipping over as it did so. The rider pushed up his goggles.

'Millicent?' he called.

She waved and ran across to him.

'Dieter! I didn't know it was you,' she said.

'Forgive me. I borrowed this motorcycle. I am not a good rider. But I must be quick.'

'What do you mean?'

'The General insists that I remain at my post at all times now. For a little while it will be impossible for me to get away. But I came because I did not want you to think . . . Look here, I will see you again once my work has been concluded.'

'When will that be?'

'Soon.'

'But how will I know when to come and meet you?'

'You must trust me, Millicent. Will you do so?'

'All right.'

They stood looking at each other.

'I must go,' he said. 'Please remember, you must not worry; I will come and find you.'

'Yes,' she said. And she could hear her heart beating. And wondered if he could hear it too.

He pulled the gauntlet off and held out his hand and she shook it.

'It won't be very long, will it?' she said.

'Not long. You give me reason to be quick. *Wiedersehn!*'

Mill watched him turn the machine and roar away. And then everything was silent.

She started back towards the stile. And it was only then that she saw the figure sitting there. And her heart began to race even faster.

'Les? Les!' she called and hurried towards him.

He slipped down and waited for her.

'How long have you been there?' she asked. 'I was just . . . '

'Yeah,' he said, 'I know what you was just—I saw you.'

'Les,' she said. 'Listen. I was only . . . He asked me the way, that's all.'

'Don't do that, Mill.'

'What?'

'Treat me like a kid. Think I'm stupid, do you?'

' 'Course I don't. Les . . . '

'What d'you think you're doing?'

'What're you talking about?'

'You know what I'm talking about. What's my sister doing knockin' about with a bloody Jerry, that's what I mean.'

'Les! I ain't doing nothing,' she said. 'We just talk, that's all. There's nothing wrong with that.'

'Can you hear yourself? Mill, he's a German.'

'Les . . . ' She touched his arm but he pulled it away.

'Don't!' he said.

'Les!'

'I don't know who you are no more!'

'Les, please listen!'

'You've changed, d'you know that?'

'I ain't, Les.'

'You have. I trusted you, Mill. You was always the one I trusted. Always. When I was a nipper and when . . . all the time, Mill. You was the one I trusted.'

'Les, he's nice,' she said desperately. 'He is! Les?'

But Les had turned away and was climbing back over the stile.

'Les!' she called. 'Les, don't tell nobody else. Please, Les.'

She went on calling but he didn't look back. And she didn't come after him. And after a while he couldn't hear her any more.

If he hadn't seen it with his own eyes he wouldn't have

believed it. Not Mill! Mill was straight as a die. He'd trusted her with his life, hadn't he? All his life. They argued all the time, 'course they did. You had to argue with Mill cos she didn't listen otherwise. But Mill was always . . . When they was nippers in London; and when they was evacuated to those evil perishers near Reading; and when they was runaways on the road, when the times were so dangerous and so hungry, traipsing from one place to another, never knowing what the next day might bring, when all they had was each other . . .

What had happened to her?

Those bloody books had happened to her, that's what! And Vera's daft ideas about everything. Making her think she was somebody else. Well, she wasn't! She was his sister, that's who she was. And he was her brother. And . . . there was something else. He was sure he'd seen that Jerry somewhere before. But where could it have been?

Les picked up a stick and hurled it angrily into the trees.

A wood pigeon thumped away into the depths of the wood and the stick clattered down noisily through the bare branches.

Chapter 7

Frank found Les sitting by the oak at the top of the lane which was where they always met. His friend's hands were rammed up into his sleeves and he was hunched against the trunk of the tree.

Frank laughed. 'You look frozen stiff,' he said. 'En't you got your newspapers on?' But Les didn't rise to his bait. 'Les?' he said. 'What's the matter?'

Les shrugged.

'Les, what is it?' He had never seen his friend looking so miserable.

'Nuffin'.'

'Something's up. I'm not silly.'

'Look, Frank . . . ' Les hesitated. How could he explain? How could he even begin to tell him that Mill, that his sister . . . And then he remembered what Alec had said about the gun. 'Look, Frank, fact is I'd tell you if I could,' he said, 'but it's a thing about myself—a private thing, all right?'

''Course. 'Course, it is,' he said. 'If that's what you want. Listen, come on down Nan's and get warm. It's too cold to mooch about.'

It was one of those dark winter days when it hardly seems to get light at all. Not that Nan was bothered. The darkness never bothered her when she was sitting in her favourite place beside the kitchen fire. She would sit there for hours. Sometimes Edith would come and sit opposite with some sewing and they would exchange the occasional observation or piece of news. Though that was rarer now since Len had come back. Otherwise Nan was happy sitting alone and peering into the fire. She had so much to remember. And she loved to watch the memories come and go among the glowing embers. It was the same corner where she had sat as a girl when it had been her parents' cottage. And she had sat there years later as a young wife with her husband, Pat. And then with her own children, with Bill and Edith, listening to the stories Pat found for them in the flames. Oh, there was no story-teller like Pat Tate. Pat who'd brought the picture of Garibaldi with him when he'd first come tramping over the hills from Ireland. And she sat there remembering now. Remembering the recent terrible years which had brought more changes with them than anyone had ever known or could ever have imagined. So many changes! These days Change was the only thing you could be sure of! Hour by hour you never knew what was round the corner.

Like this afternoon. A few words from a stranger had made her tired heart beat as proudly as she could ever remember. She'd have bought every brush in Stan Crompton's case if she'd had the money. Just to thank him.

She looked up as Frank and Les came in. 'Don't go making yourselves comfortable,' she said.

'Nan! It's cold out there. We've come in for a warm.'

'Never mind that. I've had another visit from Mr Crompton.'

'What's he want?' said Frank. 'I don't like him coming round here, Nan.'

'He wants you to do a little job for him,' she said.

'For him? We don't have to, do we, Nan?'

'He said you came highly recommended. Shut that door for us, will you, Les,' she said. 'Only I can feel a bit of a draught.'

'Recommended?' said Frank, as Les closed the door to the hall. 'Who by?'

'Apparently Mr Sims told him he couldn't have done it without you.'

Frank and Les looked at each other uneasily. 'Done what?'

'You don't have to look like that,' she said. And smiled. 'I know your secret. I know all about it. I know it was you two helped Mr Sims with Ted's bomb. Mr Sims told Mr Crompton and he told me.'

'He told Crompton!' exclaimed Frank. 'But, Nan, Crompton's . . . He's . . . '

'He ain't what any of us think he is, Frank. Stan Crompton's here to help us.'

'Help us?'

'Help us what?' said Les.

'He's been sent,' said Nan.

'Sent?'

'Yes. And about time too.'

'You mean . . . What, like a . . . ? He's an agent!' said Les suddenly. 'He is, isn't he, Mrs Tate? He's come to help us pay them back! Say he has, Mrs Tate!'

'Hold on, Les,' said Frank, 'just hold on.' And was surprised how suddenly his friend seemed to have changed his tune about fighting back. 'We don't know anything about him.'

'Frank,' said Nan, 'there's times when some things has to be took on trust. Which is just what the Nasties don't want us to do. That's the way they do it. Keeping people on their own. Frightening people into doing each other down, into not trusting each other, into telling tales and betraying each other. That way we defeat ourselves. En't that right?'

'I s'pose so.'

'Stan Crompton's putting people in touch, Frank. Getting people together. That's what's been crippling us all this time—not knowing we wasn't alone.'

'That's just what you said, Frank,' said Les.

'I know. But we don't know anything about him.'

'But he knows plenty about us,' said Nan.

'What?' demanded Frank. 'What does he know? What Mr Sims told him, that's all.'

'He knew about me.'

'What do you mean?'

'And the bike.'

'What about it?'

'He knew it was me that ran the messages, Frank. He knew where I took them and he knew who to. Mr Sims couldn't have told him that.'

'Messages, Mrs Tate?' said Les.

She nodded.

'For the Resistance?'

'You never worked for the Resistance, did you?' said Frank.

'And I still would,' she said, 'if the chance come my way and these legs of mine wasn't in such a state.'

Frank stared at her. 'Nan . . . You? You were a courier?'

Nan smiled. 'That's the posh word for it, I believe.'

'Nan, why didn't you tell me?'

'Same reason you couldn't tell me what you was doing, Frank. The less anyone knows the less they've got to tell.'

'I wouldn't have told.'

'Not willingly,' Nan said gravely. 'But the Nasties don't ask you politely. You're not a child any more. You know the way these things are done. You know what they did at Middelbury and what they do up and down this country every hour of the night and day.'

'So we was all . . . we was all sort of doing our bit at the same time and never knew it,' said Les. 'We was all helping Ted Naylor get the bomb to the Hall.'

Nan nodded. 'We was, Les.'

'And none of us knew.'

'Well, now we do. And I daresay one or two others do too. And Stan Crompton's the man who's told us. There were names he knew; all sorts of things. He's the true article.'

'What does he want us to do?' asked Les.

'He wants you up at Myrtle Lodge, where him and Mr Sims lodge.'

'Come on, Frank,' said Les and was already halfway to the door.

But Frank didn't move. 'I don't know what to say, Nan,' he said.

She reached out and took his hand. 'You don't have to say anything. This news has made me happier than I can say. I'm so proud of you.' She looked up to where Les was waiting. 'I'm proud of you both. Now get yourselves off up Myrtle Lodge. Frank?'

'What?'

'Consider Garibaldi!'

The samples case containing the wireless had been placed in the middle of the table. They were in Mr Sims's room but it was Stan Crompton who was doing the talking.

'It can't be me who takes it,' he said, 'they're watching the car.'

'You mean they suspect you?' said Sims a little anxiously.

'Not specially. But the car's conspicuous. I can't risk being stopped and searched. That case has got to be with the partisans the day after tomorrow.'

'Where?' said Frank.

'Middelbury. Or on the road somewhere nearby. That's all they'll tell me.'

'Let me take it,' said Les.

'No,' said Crompton, 'not you, Les.'

'But I know all the short-cuts.'

'You'd be too out of the ordinary. A boy with a case wandering the countryside? No, that would be bound to attract attention.' Crompton looked at Frank. 'But a boy on a bicycle wouldn't seem suspicious, would he?'

'A bicycle?' said Frank.

Crompton nodded. 'Your grandmother tells me there's one available.'

'Nan's bike?'

'What do you say? It's your decision, of course. And I won't lie to you, if you're caught . . . well, you know as well as I do what would happen if they caught you.'

'No, look here, Crompton, it shouldn't be Tate,' said Sims. 'It should be someone . . . I mean, I suppose I could go if . . . '

'No!' Frank interrupted him. 'No, I'll go. And, don't worry, they won't catch me!'

'Good lad!' Crompton reached for his case. 'I'm going to have to let them know you're coming pronto.'

'You're not going to broadcast from this room, are you?' asked Sims.

'It'll be short,' said Crompton. 'They won't be able to get a decent fix on me.'

'They're listening then?' said Les.

'Oh, yes. All the bally time.' Crompton took off his watch and placed it beside the open case.

'What's that for?' asked Frank.

'You can lose your sense of time when you're wired to these things. Never exceed five minutes under any circumstances. In fact I don't want to be on the air more than a minute if I can help it.' He took a well-thumbed paperback book from his pocket, selected a page and placed that too beside the case. 'Now then, Les, you put an ear to the door for me,' he said. 'We don't want the ladies coming in unexpectedly. And keep talking, right? About anything at all.' Crompton laughed. 'I know, tell the lads about your hobby, Professor. Tell them about those ruins of yours!'

Sims pushed his fingers through his hair irritably. 'It's not a hobby, Crompton!' he said, as Stan began to tap away at the Morse-key.

'What ruins, sir?' said Frank.

'It's nothing really, Tate. I'm . . . the fact is I'm collating information about the villa at Patfield.' Sims pulled back the cloth which he'd placed over his papers before Crompton and the boys had arrived.

'Is all that about Patfield?' said Frank.

'Oh, yes. Patfield's one of the finest examples of its kind in . . . well, in north-west Europe. I'm doing it for Mr Underwood and his wife. For their son, actually; the one who was killed. Henry Underwood was something of an expert on the matter. He took all the photographs.'

'And what's that—a painting?' said Les, picking up one of the photos from the table.

'No,' said Sims; 'no, that's a mosaic. And a particularly wonderful example. A floor. It's virtually intact. And exceptionally fine.'

'What's she doing?'

'The figure with the flowers and basket of fruit is Proserpina, Kore, or Persephone in the Greek origin of the myth,' Sims explained. 'She was the daughter of Demeter, Ceres in the Roman version. I'm sorry, these names can be rather confusing. Proserpina is returning from her seasonal absence in the Underworld. She's bringing back fruitfulness and fertility to the world. While she's away, as you can imagine, the earth is a rather bleak place.'

'Where did you say she come from?' said Les.

'From the Underworld.'

'She looks like she's just stepped through the door, don't she?'

'She doesn't half look pleased with herself,' said Frank.

'She does, doesn't she?' Sims smiled. 'I sometimes think that she's an especially hopeful figure for the awful times we live in. Light emerging finally from the darkness, as it were. Spring from winter. Life, as it were, emerging from death.'

'I say! No need to be morbid, old man,' said Crompton, pulling off his headphones. He checked his watch. 'Just over fifty seconds. We're safe enough with that.' He closed the book and was about to put it back in his pocket when Frank said:

'*The Sidewinder?* My dad used to read Westerns. Is it good?'

'This? I've no idea.' Crompton winked. 'It's not strictly for reading, if you know what I mean.'

'Is it a code book?'

'That sort of thing.' Crompton closed the case and snapped it shut. 'Our friends elsewhere will now be informed that you're coming, Frank Tate. So I suggest you nip along and sort out that bike. I'll be in touch with you later to arrange the pick up.'

Frank and Les started for the door.

'By the way, you can ride a bike, I suppose?' said Crompton.

'Oh, yes,' said Frank. And looked at Les. 'Can't I?'

Les nodded. ''Course.'

''Course you can.' Crompton grinned. 'All boys can ride a bike, can't they?'

Oberleutnant Werner Lang had been finalizing the reports on the unfortunate shooting of the local child for most of the morning. Duplicate copies for this department and triplicate copies for that. The investigation was scrupulously thorough. And, he knew from experience, quite pointless. The documents would be despatched in all directions, they would be received and carefully recorded, and then they would disappear into the system for good. There seemed to be more and more paperwork like that.

'You are certain, Mainz?' he said, closing the filing cabinet.

'Yes, Oberleutnant. Less than ten minutes ago. I was out with the patrol and I came back to headquarters at once.'

'I wouldn't wish to disturb the General unnecessarily.'

'No, Oberleutnant. But he did ask me to inform him immediately if there was anything at all to report.'

The Oberleutnant frowned. He had an idea the young soldier had just put him in his place. 'Very well,' he said. 'Come this way.'

Dieter Mainz followed him along the corridor until they reached the doors of the Great Library where he was told to wait while Lang knocked and was summoned inside.

Dieter waited impatiently. He had been waiting impatiently for two days. Two days of nothing but silence. And now every second was crucial.

Finally, the door was opened and Lang beckoned him in.

Dieter saluted. And stared. He had never seen so many books. They filled the walls from floor to ceiling on all sides of a room so large it had a metal balcony running round it.

Of all the fine rooms in Shevington Hall the Great Library was the General's favourite. He had fought tooth and nail to preserve it from the signals engineers, with their drills and their endless lengths of cable. Its shelves were inexhaustible, crammed with treasures which in the two years he had occupied the Hall he had hardly even begun to discover.

He looked up from the large leather-bound book which was open on the table in front of him. 'Well, Mainz,' he said, 'Lang tells me you have something for me at last?'

'Less than ten minutes ago, Herr General.'

'Where?'

'A very brief transmission. But Paris central picked it up.'

'And?'

'I have re-drawn the triangle inside which the illegal is transmitting, Herr General.'

'And?'

'Herr General, it includes the village.'

'Shevington?'

'Yes, Herr General.'

'You mean he is on our doorstep?' Von Schreier glanced at Lang. 'Are you certain, Mainz?'

'I am certain that the village is part of the possible area of transmission, Herr General.'

'Can't you be more precise?'

'The transmission was too brief, Herr General. One of even a little more length would allow me to target him to within two hundred metres.'

'Then I want the listening-watch scrupulously maintained. By you personally, Mainz. You are the expert. And the road patrol must be on permanent stand-by. See to that, Werner. Thank you, Mainz; you may return to your post. And, Mainz?'

'Herr General?'

'Well done. Let him see himself out, Werner.' When the corporal had gone von Schreier rose to his feet and walked over to the window. 'The hyenas can smell blood,' he said. 'Do you think they have heard the news from the Eastern Front?'

'Almost certainly, Herr General.'

'And that is bound to encourage resistance. However futile.' The General took off his spectacles and rubbed his forehead wearily. 'I am a soldier, Werner, not a policeman. I fight other soldiers not civilians who do not know when they are beaten.'

'They cannot win, Herr General.'

'No, Werner, of course not. But we could lose.'

Rose waited as long as she could. Her mother seemed to take forever deciding to go down to The Green.

As soon as Edie left she got up quickly from the table.

Nan looked round from her chair beside the fire. 'You all right, Rose?'

'Yes, Nan. I've just got to . . . I'm just popping upstairs for a minute.'

There was no answer when she knocked.

'Dad?' she called softly.

He was sitting at the window as usual and didn't seem aware that she'd come in. But she knew he was.

'Dad? Please, don't. I didn't mean it; I didn't mean what I said. You know I didn't.'

‘I think you did, Rose,’ he replied coldly.

‘Dad, I wouldn’t want you to be in that camp still. I wouldn’t want that. How can you think I would?’

‘En’t that what you said?’

‘No. I said . . . ’

He turned from the window and looked at her. ‘Go on. What did you say?’

‘I said you might as well be. Sitting up here the way you do. Never going out anywhere. Being on your own all the time. Dad, you’re home now. You’re our dad again.’

He looked at her for a moment and then turned back to the window. She watched him silently, trying to think of what she could say to him. She saw him reach into the pocket of his overcoat and take out a piece of paper.

‘Here,’ he said. ‘Go on, take it.’

‘What is it?’ she said.

‘My identity papers.’

‘Dad . . . ’

‘They took everything else at Dunkirk. Did you know that? They take everything you’ve got when you’re captured. Cos you don’t need anything. Not when you’re nobody. Not when you don’t exist any more.’

‘Dad . . . ’

‘We were the forgotten, Rose; we were forgotten men. Right from the start,’ he said, his voice rising. ‘It took me a long time to twig that. We were forgotten right from the start. We were the ones who held the perimeter while the boats came and took the rest of ’em back to Blighty. We were the ones they left behind. No one came for us.’

She looked down at the creased document in her hand. And up again from the photo there to the gaunt, anxious man sitting on the chair by the window.

‘They took everything!’ he said. ‘That’s all I’ve got left, Rose!’

'Don't you dare say that!' she replied angrily. 'Don't you dare!'

He was startled by her anger. 'Don't . . . don't tell me what to do, girl.'

'That's just what I will do. You've got us,' she said. 'We've waited and hoped and never forgotten you. All of us. You think we en't had hard times and all? Cos we have. There en't many who haven't. There's thousands have been left with nothing and nobody. You think our ma en't suffered and struggled.'

'She left Swindon! She left our house and came here,' he said bitterly. 'That was our house.'

She stared at him. It was true: he didn't know. He didn't know what the German bombers had done. 'Dad,' she said, 'honestly, ma didn't have no choice.'

'Yes she did. She chose to bring you here. And there was no need. That was our home. I en't even got that now. I en't even got a place to go back to. To call my own.'

'Dad, she done the right thing. Dad, please? It's nice here. It is!'

But he had turned his back again and was once more gazing from the window.

'Look, I've got to go, Dad. To go to work. Dad, we want you home with us properly. I don't know how else to tell you.' And leaving the identity papers on the bed, she hurried out.

She went downstairs and collected her coat. As she went out of the back door she was surprised to see Nan and Frank and his pal, Les. Frank was wheeling Nan's bike.

'Nan?' she said in alarm. 'You're never going out on it!'

Nan laughed. 'Don't be so daft, Rose. No,' she said, 'it's for Frank. Seems a pity to let the old thing rust away.'

'I didn't know you could ride a bike, Frank,' she said.

'I can't,' he said. 'Not yet.'

'You take care, then,' she said. 'See you, later.'

She started down the lane. And she hadn't gone far when Frank and the bike wobbled past. Les was holding the saddle and running behind him and the two of them were laughing at the tops of their voices.

Chapter 8

Edie Worth placed the teacup on the window ledge next to her husband.

She was pleased Rose had made the effort to talk to him the other day. Though what she'd told her he'd said worried her. Still, maybe if they both kept trying he'd come round eventually.

'It's starting to thaw,' she said. 'Why don't you come downstairs, eh, Len? We could go for a stroll. We don't have to go into the village if you don't want to.'

'I don't,' he said. 'I've no wish to be stared at and whispered over like a damned freak-show.'

'Then what about a bit of a walk up the lane?'

But Len didn't reply.

'At least come down and sit in the kitchen with us, eh?'

'He's off on that damned bike again,' he said, peering out into the back garden. 'And that cockney's with him.'

'Les?' she said, looking over his shoulder.

'How come your mother give her bike to Frank and not to our Colin?'

'I don't know,' she said. 'It doesn't matter, does it?'

She watched Frank remove the tarpaulin from the bicycle and wheel it down the path. But she couldn't hear what Nan was saying to him.

'You'll take care, Frank, won't you?' said Nan.

''Course. I'll be all right. I've got the hang of it now.'

'Riding the bike is the least of it. By rights it ought to be me was going.'

'I'm going for you, Nan,' he said. 'For all of us. Consider Garibaldi, eh?'

'And come home safe.'

'He's going shopping for Nan, that's all,' said Edie, as she saw her mother hand Frank the basket and watched him fix it on the handlebars. And then Nan kissed Frank on the cheek. Now why on earth was she doing that?

'I wish I was coming with you, Frank,' said Les, when they reached the gate. And offered his hand. 'Good luck.'

Frank grinned and shook it. 'See you later.'

Les watched him head off up the lane. He stood watching long after Frank had turned out of sight. He would have given anything to be the one on that bike. It should have been him. Didn't he have more reason than anyone to be having a go at the bloody Germans?

The car was parked not far from the crossroads. The bonnet was raised and the driver was leaning inside. He looked up as cycle and rider approached.

'Need a hand?' asked Frank, stopping beside him.

'What's that, old man? No. Kind of you to offer but I think I know what the trouble is. And I daresay you've got better things to do. Take care, though, these lanes can be treacherous in weather like this.'

Frank picked up the samples case which was leaning against the running-board and placed it quickly in the basket. 'All the best,' he said.

'And you, old man. Yes, indeed.'

The back roads below the Downs had been lonely places even in peacetime and Frank met no one as he rode along. The time and miles sped by and within twenty minutes or so he wasn't far from Patfield Palace. But as the ruin came into view he gripped the brakes and slithered to a halt. A Wehrmacht staff car was parked at the side of the road and beside it stood two German officers. And they'd seen him. He had no choice but to go on.

The one with the camera waved him down and walked over to him.

'We are looking for Patfield Palace,' he said. 'These are the ruins, yes?'

Frank nodded.

'*Wir haben den richtigen Ort gefunden, Herr General!*' the German called to his companion.

The General! Frank had often seen von Schreier in the back of his car as he travelled backwards and forwards from the Hall but he hadn't recognized him standing in the snow wrapped in his heavy coat. But it was all right: the General didn't seem interested in him. He seemed much more interested in the ruins. The young officer, however, was another matter.

'You are travelling far?' he enquired, looking at the neat, leather case in the basket on Frank's handlebars.

'Me? Yes,' said Frank. 'Yes, I am.'

'You have chosen a bad day. I used to ride a bicycle when I was your age. It is great fun. But this is not good weather for doing so.'

'I know.'

'Your journey must be important.'

'It is. I'm . . . I'm going to see someone.' They stood facing each other for a moment or two. Then: 'Can I go now?' said Frank. 'Only . . . '

The officer smiled. 'Of course. And good bicycling!'

Frank pedalled away; he hoped without too much urgency.

Werner Lang watched him go then walked back to where the General was waiting.

Von Schreier had discovered the folio of drawings in the Great Library only that morning: a series of fine, early nineteenth century ink-sketches illustrating local sites of antiquarian interest. And among them were several sheets depicting the remains of what seemed to have once been a considerable Roman villa. He had immediately called for his car.

'Even under the snow this site is superb, Werner!' he said, shaking his head in admiration.

After what he reckoned must have been another hour

Frank began the ascent of the long hill beyond which he was sure Middelbury must lie. He had passed this way only once before, when he had walked from Seabourne to Nan's not long after the Invasion. His memory of Middelbury was of a Downland village much like any other: a small church faced with flints, a pub, the village shop, and a huddle of houses strung out along the road that followed the foot of the hills. But when he reached the crest what he saw made him stop and get down from the saddle.

The church with its lych-gate and squat tower was all that was left; it stood alone, like a terrible, solitary signpost pointing to the desolation all around it. As he looked down on the empty, snow-bound landscape with its smooth white mounds where houses had once been, and the occasional fragments of dark wall, stripped to the brick by the wind and protruding like tombstones, he felt as though he was looking down on a graveyard.

It was just as people said: the Germans had burned Middelbury to the ground.

This had been Ted Naylor's village. That was why they had done this terrible thing. Because Ted had fought back.

He wheeled the bike slowly down the hill. When he reached the lych-gate he paused and looked around. It was like a battlefield. But there had been no battle here. No bloody struggle one against the other. Instead, innocent people had been murdered out of hand and the rest herded away to no one knew where and disappeared forever. He shivered. He could feel them there. In that terrible, silent emptiness he could feel their presence. You couldn't call them ghosts, not in broad daylight, and, besides, they made no sound or gesture, they didn't moan or wail, and they made no attempt to approach him, but they were there. They stood at a distance, crowding what must have been the pavements each side of that village street, the old and the young, men and women and children, gazing at him helplessly.

All he remembered was a strong hand clamped over his mouth and a blindfold being knotted tightly over his eyes.

'Bring it with you!' he heard someone say, as his arms were pinioned and the bike was snatched from his grip.

When his feet next touched the ground he was stumbling on slippery, stone steps. He heard a door being closed and bolted and breathed a damp, musty smell as though he was underground.

'Don't touch the blindfold,' said a voice.

'It's all here,' said another.

'Good. You've done well, lad,' said the first voice. 'Any problems on the way?'

'Are you . . . ?'

'Never you mind who we are. I asked you if you had any trouble?'

'No. Well, not a problem. I saw General von Schreier,' he said.

Both voices spoke at once. 'Von Schreier? Where?'

'His car was parked next to Patfield Palace.'

'What the hell was he doing there?'

'Just looking,' said Frank. 'Him and another one. The other one asked me about the ruins.'

'You spoke to them?'

'I had to. He stopped me.'

'With that case right under their noses?'

'There was nothing I could do about it.'

'What did you tell them?'

'Nothing.'

'Did you now?' The speaker laughed. 'You're a cool young blighter.'

'It'd better be him who comes next time,' said the other voice.

'Next time?' said Frank.

'When we're finished with the case it has to go back where it came from. Tell your man to send you in two days' time. You're to come by the same road at the same sort of time just like you did today. I suppose now you'd like your reward?'

'I haven't done it for that,' said Frank indignantly.

'Well, I'll give you one anyway. How would you like some news from Stalingrad?'

'Stalingrad?' There'd been less and less news from Stalingrad. When the Russian city had first been besieged the walls of The Office had been hung with maps and daily bulletins of the imminent triumph of the German Sixth Army and its allies. That had been months ago. Since then the maps had been taken down and the reports had been fewer and fewer and everyone had assumed that it was all over and that the Nazis had captured it like so many other Soviet cities along the Eastern Front. 'Have they taken it?' asked Frank.

'No, son, they haven't. They've been taken. Good and proper. The Russkies have broken the siege. They've taken thousands of prisoners. A whole damned army. It's a great victory. The first of many.'

'Time's getting on,' said the other voice.

'We're going to leave you here,' said the first. 'I want you to wait a minute or two and then take off your blindfold. Close the door carefully behind you. Your bike's outside. Get on it and go. And don't look back. Can I trust you to do what I say?'

'Yes,' said Frank.

'Two days' time, remember?'

He heard footsteps, the door opened and closed, and then there was silence. He waited. Then he pulled off the blindfold and looked round the gloomy chamber in which he found himself. Some light filtered in from a narrow fan-shaped window at ceiling level. The walls were old and damp and along their sides were several deep niches. Each contained a stone coffin. He was in the crypt of the church. He ran up the steps and pulled open the door then closed it carefully behind him. He made his way down the gravel path and out under the lych-gate. Then he rode, as fast as he could, up the hill and away from the village.

At the top of the hill he stopped and risked one glance

back the way he had come. There was no one to be seen. Whoever had collected the wireless from him had melted back into the snow as easily and silently as they had emerged from it. Or perhaps they had been ghosts too. Like the other spirits that roamed that terrible place.

He turned and started down the road for home. He pedalled hard, frantically, and then lifted his feet from the pedals and let the bike take him. 'Nan?' he called, as the hedges flew by. 'Can you hear me, Nan? They've been beaten! They can be beaten, Nan! We've done it!' And the wind rushed past him and into his mouth and the old bike bucked and clattered until it seemed it would shake to pieces. But it didn't. It went on rolling. Free! Free as a bird.

He was still a good twelve miles from home when the front wheel twisted beneath him and sent him into the side of the hedge. When he picked himself up and inspected the tyre he found that it was punctured. There was no question of riding any further. There was nothing else for it—he was going to have to walk.

It would be dark in an hour or so. There was no way he'd be back before curfew.

The light was fading and there really wasn't much point remaining at his desk. Peter Sims collected the photographs and notes together and bundled them into his briefcase.

The sound of a vehicle arriving outside made him look up. He saw the driver get out and open the rear door of the silver-grey staff-car. The two figures who emerged came through the gates and across the empty playground. Sims hurried out of the office and was there to meet them as they arrived at the foot of the steps.

'Is something wrong?' he asked.

Oberleutnant Lang smiled. 'Mr Sims?'

'I am Sims.'

'General von Schreier would like a word with you.'

'With me? You'd better come inside.'

'This is an informal visit, Herr Sims,' said the General, as he took the chair opposite. 'Sit down, please. I have come to pick your brains.'

'I'm afraid I know very little about military matters.'

'And are a happier man for your ignorance, I'm sure. No, Herr Sims, it is your schoolmaster's hat I require you to wear for me. I'm told you read Classics at Cambridge?'

'Who told you that?'

'You have no secrets from us, Herr Sims.' Von Schreier smiled. 'Don't look so alarmed. These details are a matter of record, no more than that. There is nothing very sinister about it.' The General had been about to remove his gloves but instead he looked round the room. 'Have you no heating here?' he said.

'No. No,' said Sims. 'I've been waiting for coal for some weeks. That's the reason I've had to send the pupils home.'

'Make a note of that, Werner. I will see what can be done for you, Herr Sims.'

'Thank you.'

'Now, Herr Sims, Patfield Palace?'

'I beg your pardon?'

'Patfield Palace, Herr Sims.'

It was a moment or two before Peter Sims could collect himself. 'The um . . . the ruin?'

'Yes. What can you tell me about it?'

'Very . . . very little. Other than the fact that . . . it's a . . . or rather, is said to be, a Roman villa,' Sims heard himself say.

'But it is called a "palace". And it appears that there has been some excavation there of a rather amateur kind.'

'Archaeology isn't my speciality, I'm afraid.' Sims ran his fingers nervously through his hair. Why? Why was he lying to this extremely powerful man, a man with the power of life and death, a man with so much blood on his hands? 'I've visited the villa, of course,' he said. 'Once or twice.'

'I have seen drawings of a fine mosaic floor. You have seen this on your visits?'

'Yes.'

'And it is particularly fine?'

'It's quite impressive, yes. If you care for that sort of thing.'

'I do, Herr Sims. We are not all barbarians, you know. And it occurs to me that perhaps when the spring comes it might be possible to organize a fuller excavation of the site. Would that interest you—as a classical scholar?'

'As I've explained, I'm not an archaeologist and . . . '

'And if this floor is as fine as they say it is,' the General continued enthusiastically, 'someone should take steps to ensure its preservation, don't you think?'

'What do you mean?'

'I mean that to leave such an historic treasure to deteriorate would be an act of wanton criminality. Far better for it to be removed to a place of safety. We have museums in Germany which specialize in such matters.'

'A museum?'

'Our curators and conservation experts have considerable experience. It would be done with great care.'

Sims got to his feet. 'The care that might be taken is altogether irrelevant, General von Schreier!' he heard himself say angrily. 'It is the fact that you'd even consider such an act of vandalism that I find astonishing. You have robbed us of our present and now it seems you're trying to take away our past as well.' He stood, running his fingers through his hair, and waiting for the reaction he knew must come.

But von Schreier simply pursed his lips thoughtfully. Then he stood up. 'I am disappointed in you, Herr Sims. I hoped we might co-operate in this matter. I hope we still may. The past has much to teach us,' he said; 'especially a nation as successful as the Romans. I feel sure that, on reflection, you will see the sense of my proposal. Good day. And I will see what can be done about your coal supplies.'

Sims watched them cross the playground. The man meant it. Every word of it. That urbane, educated, and apparently civilized man clearly believed that such an action would not be the action of a barbarian! Of a vandal! Of a . . . He really believed it. Dear God, what could one do against such people?

The darkness, the absolute darkness, of the countryside at night was still something Stan Crompton found alarming. Even with the carpet of snow there was scarcely light enough to see any distance.

Stan had called at Nan Tate's not long before dusk expecting Frank to be there. That was the plan. For Frank to have come directly to Myrtle Lodge would have been too dangerous. Dangerous? It was all dangerous. Even standing here in this hedge was dangerous! Stan knew he should have been back at Myrtle Lodge himself by now, so long after curfew. But . . . but there was still a chance the boy would turn up. Wasn't there?

Yes. If he hadn't already been taken. If it hadn't all gone wrong. If the radio and the boy weren't already in the hands of the Gestapo. Then what? There was only so much time one could afford to hang about before covering one's tracks and clearing out. Those were the rules.

Sound carried on these still nights. That was something at least. And he had good warning of the approaching patrol when it was still some way away. Time enough for him to duck even further behind the hedge opposite the cottage. And hold his breath.

The headlights of the lorry came glaring along the dark lane and it roared past, its tyres hissing on the wet snow. They were obviously in a hurry to get back to their warm canteen.

Stan sighed. It was no good. It was time to call it a

day. He stepped from the shelter of the hedge and stood taking a last look along the lane. Which was when he heard it: a rustling on the other side of the hedge. That was something else Stan couldn't get used to: how full of noises the darkness always seemed to be. Things you couldn't see, moving about somewhere. It was enough to give you the creeps.

They were as startled as each other when the moment came: the boy who came through the gate with the bicycle over his shoulder and the nervous man standing transfixed in the road beyond.

'Frank Tate!' said Stan, clutching his chest. 'Thank the Lord it's you.'

'Mr Crompton? What are you doing here?'

'I'm waiting for you, that's what.'

'I had a puncture. I had to stick to the fields once it was dark.'

'Good man, good man! You made the delivery?'

Frank nodded. 'And I'm supposed to collect it again the day after tomorrow.'

'You're a hero, that's what you are. Now get inside. They're worried sick about you. And, Frank?' Stan held out his hand. 'Well done.'

Frank leaned the bike against the wash-house wall and covered it carefully with the tarpaulin. Nan would be bound to have a puncture-kit and he would set to repairing that front tyre first thing in the morning.

He pushed open the kitchen door. Nan was nodding in her chair beside the fire. There was an oil-lamp glowing on the table where his aunt Edith was sitting with Rose next to her. And sitting opposite them was Len Worth.

His aunt turned as Frank came in. 'Frank!' she exclaimed. 'Frank, wherever have you been?'

Rose got up and hurried across to him. 'Look at you,' she said, 'you're soaking wet. Frank, where have you been?'

'Well, boy?' Len Worth stood up. 'What have you got to say for yourself?'

'I had a puncture.'

'And do you know what time it is? Well, do you?'

'There wasn't anything I could do about it,' said Frank.

'Frank? Frank, is that you?' Nan had woken. 'Frank, my dear,' she said, getting to her feet unsteadily. 'I must have dozed off. Come here. Thank the Lord, you're safe.'

'Puncture, Nan,' he said, taking her hand. 'But everything's all right.'

'Oh, it's all right, is it?' said Len angrily. 'Do you know the penalty for being caught out after curfew? We could all have suffered the consequences if you'd been taken, do you know that? Yes—you know it all right but you don't give a damn, do you? And don't look at me like that.' Len placed himself between Frank and the door. 'You're not leaving this room until you've told me where you've been all this time.'

'Leave him be, Len,' said Nan wearily. 'You can see the boy's worn out. You get upstairs, Frank, and get yourself dry.'

'He'll do no such thing. He'll go nowhere till I've had an answer.'

'Please, Dad? Please,' said Rose. 'It's late and . . . '

They all waited, watching the man by the door.

'I want an answer,' said Len in a voice that was scarcely audible even in that tiny room. 'I want a few things sorted out. Now.'

'Listen to me, Len,' said Nan. 'Where Frank's been is his business. I'm willing to take his word he had a puncture. That could happen to anyone. Frank wouldn't put us in danger if he could help it. He's not that sort. And he's not a child any more. And if you spent a bit less time sat on your behind up at that window you might get to know him better and realize that. You might get to realize a lot of things if you did that. Frank, give me a hand upstairs.'

Frank took her arm and they began to walk towards the door. When they reached it Len moved aside.

As they made their way along the hall Frank whispered: 'They've been beaten, Nan. The Russians have beaten them good and proper.'

He felt her hand tighten on his arm. 'All that matters is that you're safe, child.'

They climbed the stairs slowly. And found Colin sitting in the darkness halfway up. He was shivering. He looked at Frank and then at his grandmother. 'Nan,' he said anxiously, 'why was he shouting?'

'It's all right now, Colin,' she replied. 'You go on down and get warm.'

Len Worth stood in front of the fire with his back to his wife and daughter. As Colin reached the doorway he heard him say: 'I'll take no more of this. I've had enough. We're going home.'

'Len!' 'Dad!' said Edie and Rose together.

'Did you hear me?'

'Back to Swindon, Len?'

'That's home as far as I remember it. I won't stay in this house any longer and nor will you.'

'But, Dad . . . You can't! You can't make us go back.'

He turned to face them. 'I won't hear another word. From anyone. We're going home. Now go to bed, all of you.'

Chapter 9

Frank peered over the blanket. The morning was bitterly cold. Despite the newspaper stuffed around the window-frames there was frost on the inside of the glass: long glittering crystals reaching across the pane like the fingers of a silver hand.

On the other side of the room Colin was sitting up in bed. He was wearing his pullover over his pyjamas and he had his woollen gloves on.

'I've been awake ages,' he said.

Frank rubbed his eyes sleepily. 'What's up?'

'It's our dad. I didn't think it would be like this when he came home, Frank. I thought he'd make things all right. But he hasn't. It's not all right—not any of it. I don't want to go back to Swindon.'

'He was in a temper, Col.'

'He doesn't understand what's happened. And Mum and Rose won't tell him. Frank?'

'What?'

'I haven't got any other cousins. Except you.'

The door opened and Edie came in. Her face was pale and her eyes were red. She had been crying.

'Ma?' said Colin alarmed. 'Ma, what's up?'

She shook her head and it was a moment or two before she spoke.

'You're to get up right away,' she said. 'Something's happened.'

'Ma? Ma, what?' said Colin anxiously. 'Ma, what is it?'

'Your nan's gone,' she said quietly.

'Where?' said Frank.

'Just get dressed, the both of you.'

Frank threw aside the blanket and jumped out of bed. 'She can't have,' he said. 'She can hardly walk. She can't have gone!' But there was something about Edie's stillness that made him stop. Something that choked off any more words before he could say them.

'It must have been in the night,' she said. 'That's how I found her this morning. Like she was asleep.'

'But she . . . ' He shook his head. Was that what his aunt meant? Nan was . . . Not Nan. That didn't make sense. There was some mistake. No, Nan couldn't be . . . She would be there when they went downstairs. She was always there.

'Get dressed. Quick now.'

Rose and Len were already in the kitchen.

'There's things will have to be organized,' said Edie. 'Rose, you're to go and fetch Mrs Follett. And I'm going down to The Office to make the arrangements. Len, get that fire lit. And you boys . . . just keep out of mischief.'

Frank and Colin sat in the kitchen while Len Worth struggled with the fire. Rose came back with Mrs Follett who went upstairs. When Edie returned about an hour later, Mrs Follett came downstairs and Frank heard her tell his aunt quietly: 'I've made her presentable. She's a loss to us all, Mrs Worth.'

Edie turned to Frank and Colin. 'Would you like to see her?' she asked.

Frank nodded.

'If Frank's going to,' said Colin uncertainly.

She took them upstairs and pushed open Nan's door.

They stood together in the bare room: there was only a wardrobe and the old metal bed with the small table next to it, on which someone had placed a prayer-book. That must have been Mrs Follett, thought Frank; he couldn't remember seeing it there before. Nan was in bed. She looked preoccupied. She had a cloth tied round her jaw for some reason, like she had toothache. Like in the comics. He wanted to touch her fingers where her hands lay together on the faded counterpane but he felt that in doing so he might distract her from whatever it was she seemed to be concentrating on so hard.

'Frank?' Colin whispered. 'Frank, is that Granfer Tate?' He was looking up at the picture above the bed: the bearded man in the red shirt staring into the dawn.

'No,' said Frank, 'it's Garibaldi.'

'Oh.'

Edie called to them quietly and they went out and she shut the door.

'Frank?' she said. But he shook his head and walked away down the stairs. He went through the kitchen where Len was still struggling with the fire. His uncle looked up and seemed about to speak but Frank didn't stop. He walked out into the back garden and round to the wash-house where the bike stood beneath its tarpaulin. And then he burst into uncontrollable tears.

People came to the cottage all that day.

Les came. He stood next to Frank and said that he didn't know what to say. And Frank said that it didn't matter and thanked him for coming in a strangely formal way. But that seemed to be the way things were done. Everybody seemed to be talking like that.

They all came: Mr Underwood and his wife; Farmer Follett and his family, with Ned proudly wearing a sling round his arm; Mr Sims, who brought formal condolences from the Misses Elliott; and Miss Meacher; Vera Thrale came with Mill, who carried the wreath of evergreens Vera had made; Betty Firth, an old enemy but now distressed more than she could understand at Nan's passing. And later that afternoon some men came with a coffin and carried it upstairs.

Not long after that Stan Crompton arrived. 'I've only just heard,' he said. 'A terrible loss, Frank.'

'Mr Crompton, the funeral's tomorrow.'

Crompton frowned. 'Tomorrow? You're supposed to make that collection tomorrow.'

'I can't, Mr Crompton.'

'No, you can't,' said the salesman, ''course you can't.'

'It doesn't matter, I'll go,' said Les.

'No,' said Crompton; 'it'll have to be me. I'll take the car. What time is the funeral, Frank?'

'Half past ten.'

'I'll be there for the funeral. That's only right and proper. And then I'll drive to Middelbury.'

'Take me with you,' said Les. 'I can show you the way.'

'It's a straight road.'

'Let me come, Mr Crompton, please! I know that countryside inside out.'

Les was still pleading with the salesman as he and Crompton walked away.

Frank stayed outside most of the day. The cottage with its comings and goings was too much for him.

He was down by the old chicken run when he heard Colin say:

'I looked him up, Frank.'

He turned and found his cousin standing on the path nearby. He was clutching his encyclopaedia.

'Who, Col?'

'He's in here.'

'Who is?'

'Garibaldi. He was famous, Frank. He went about fighting tyranny. In Italy. And he went to South America as well.'

'I know.'

'Why did Nan like him specially?'

'Because he never gave up.'

'That's what she used to say, wasn't it—about not giving up? I don't want to give up, Frank. But what can we do? Dad's bound to take us back to Swindon now.'

Frank shrugged. 'I suppose.'

'You won't like it, Frank. It's not like here.'

'What are you talking about?'

'You'll have to come with us. You won't be able to stay here on your own, will you?'

Wherever he looked that day he was looking for Nan. As he mooched about the garden he half expected to see her come wheeling the bike up the path, the way she used to, red-faced from one of her expeditions, carrying the news from one place to another, fighting back. Or busy with her chickens down by the old run. Nan had loved her hens. He'd helped her feed them or collect the eggs so many times. Though not always very willingly. He was sure that if he looked hard enough he'd see her there, with a chicken perched on her shoulder as she threw them their feed. It was impossible to think she wasn't there. From the moment he'd come traipsing up the lane from Seabourne Nan had always been there.

And she was there when he did at last fall asleep that night. He remembered the nights when she had let him sit with her last thing, talking about his dad. Her Bill. Or just sitting there silently, beside the fire in the kitchen, without having to say anything at all, staring into the embers.

Farmer Follett and three other men came next morning and carried the coffin downstairs and along the lane from the cottage to the churchyard on the other side of The Green. It seemed to rest so lightly on their shoulders, Frank thought, as he followed with Edie and Rose and Colin, and Len walking behind them.

People left the queues outside The Office and Dearman's, the village shop, and stood on the pavement as Nan passed. They stood in silence; and the men took off their hats despite the cold.

A clergyman had been sent for by The Office. But Shevington Church had been closed since the invasion and despite Edith's pleas permission to open it had been refused.

As the cortège passed through the gates into the churchyard and the short ceremony began, the villagers crossed The Green and stood along the wall looking on.

'For all flesh is grass,' intoned the clergyman; 'and all the glory of man as the flower of grass. The grass withereth and the flower thereof . . . '

But Frank wasn't listening. He stood beside Colin gazing down into the chalky rectangle in which the coffin lay. And it was only then that he knew for certain Nan would not be there when they got back to the cottage. She'd gone. But not far. He was sure of that. She was away pedalling the roads around Shevington the way she had always done and always would do while he remembered her. Which would be always. She'd be there wherever he went—free as a bird. Never giving up.

'Frank?'

It was Rose and Edie. 'We're going back to the house now, Frank,' said his aunt. 'Your uncle Len's already gone. Frank, what is it? What's the matter?'

'What about Dad?' he said. 'Who's going to tell him?'

'Your dad?' Edie looked at Rose. 'But, Frank . . . ' she said.

'What?' He knew what his aunt had been about to say. He knew she'd given up all hope of ever seeing her brother again. He could see it in her face. 'Somebody's got to let him know Nan's dead,' he said.

'Yes, Frank, of course,' she said. 'Are you coming, then?'

'In a minute.'

As the churchyard began to empty even villagers who'd never spoken to Frank before came and shook his hand. It seemed very important to them to murmur their condolences. They hadn't lost Nan but whatever it was they had lost seemed to need saying.

Mr Sims, Crompton, and Les were among the last to approach him.

'She was one of the best, Frank,' said Les.

'I'm sure you'll miss her greatly, Tate,' said Sims. 'These are such bleak occasions but . . . she was, I'm sure, immensely proud of you.' He ran his fingers nervously through his hair. 'And so she should be.'

'Couldn't have put it better, old man,' said Crompton, as he in turn shook Frank's hand.

'When are you leaving?' asked Frank.

'Right away. The car's parked over the way. I don't think it should take more than a couple of hours there and back.' He nodded at Les. 'And I've got my guide with me if I get lost.'

They began to walk towards where Stan's car was parked but were stopped by the wail of approaching klaxons as two troop-carriers came speeding along the road from Shevington Hall. The lorries were followed by a motorbike and sidecar which skidded to a halt outside The Office. The sentry at the door hurried over and exchanged a few words with the rider and his passenger and the motorbike set off again in pursuit of the lorries. A crowd gathered round the sentry. And it was from this crowd that George Poole and Wally Carr emerged.

'What's going on, lads?' enquired Crompton.

'Trouble, that's what. There's been trouble down Worthing way. Somebody's derailed a train,' said Poole. 'There's soldiers everywhere.' And he and Wally ran off.

Crompton frowned. 'I don't like the sound of that.'

'What're we going to do?' said Les.

'We can't risk making the collection. Not now. It's asking to be caught.'

'But this is just the time they won't be expecting anyone to . . . '

'No,' said Crompton firmly. 'No avoidable risks. It's going to have to wait. We'll try again tomorrow morning. Meet me out at the crossroads. If you're still on?'

' 'Course I am!'

'Cheer up, old man. You'll get your chance to be a hero.'

How they'd gawped at the POW! They'd looked at him as if he was something from a blessed sideshow. Well, let 'em stare. He'd done his duty. He'd done what Edie asked him to and seen the old woman to her rest. And now it was time to go home.

Mind you, there were one or two of the villagers who had been what you could call sympathetic. One or two who'd asked after him respectfully. With the respect due to a soldier. One or two who'd said as how it couldn't be easy coming back after so long. And he'd answered 'em and told 'em just how hard it was! They didn't know the half of it! Let me tell you, my friends, it most definitely was not easy! Still, it was decent of 'em to enquire.

Len Worth was almost at the cottage gate when he heard the footsteps. He turned and found Colin running after him up the lane.

'Dad? Dad, wait!'

The boy looked upset. 'Slow down,' Len called. 'You'll fall and hurt yourself. Slow down, boy!'

'I've got something to tell you, Dad. You've got to listen.'

'What's the matter?'

'Dad, we can't go back to Swindon. We can't!'

Len turned and tried to walk on but Colin clung to his coat.

'Please don't make us go back. Dad, we can't!'

'And I say we can, Colin,' said Len, pushing him away. 'And that's it and all about it.'

'But we can't! Cos there's nothing to go back to.'

'Don't be so damn silly, boy.'

'Dad, there isn't! It's gone. The Jerries bombed the goods yards and sheds and everything for miles around. They bombed it all flat. Our house and all . . . all of it.'

'What are you talking about?'

'Dad, it's gone. Nobody wanted to tell you cos they were frightened of upsetting you. Mrs Ward wrote to ma about it. Dad, we haven't got anywhere to go back to.'

Len Worth staggered; and would have fallen if Colin hadn't taken hold of his coat and held him up. They stood together swaying in the middle of the road.

Which was how Edie and Rose found them as they came up the lane. 'Len?' 'Dad?' they called, running towards them. 'Whatever's the matter?'

'I told him,' said Colin. 'I told him about Swindon, ma. Ma, I had to.'

'Oh, Len! Len, it's all right.' Edie stepped forward and put her arms around her husband.

'Dad,' said Rose, holding on to his ragged sleeve, 'you had to know sometime.'

He couldn't bring himself to look at them. He looked over their heads and up into the wintry sky. 'It's gone, then—all of it?' he said.

Edie nodded. 'Yes, Len.'

'They've took it all?'

'No, Len, they haven't. We've got each other,' she said. 'That's a sight more than thousands of poor devils have got. We've got each other.'

When he got back from the funeral Frank could hear the Worths talking in the kitchen.

He didn't go in. Instead, he removed the tarpaulin from Nan's bike and took another look at the front tyre.

Which was where Edie found him. 'What're you doing out here?' she asked.

He shrugged. 'Where did Nan keep the things for mending punctures?'

'Behind that toby jug on the dresser. You're not going to do that now, are you?'

'I might.'

'Look, Frank, Len and I have been talking. I know you and him haven't exactly seen eye to eye and everything but . . . We're not going back to Swindon, Frank. I've persuaded him to stay.'

'Stay where?'

'Here.' She waited for his reaction but none came. He just went on fiddling with the wheel of the bicycle. 'Frank, it's only right. This was my home; this is where me and your dad were brought up,' she said. 'Me and Len and Colin and Rose are staying. And I want you to stay along with us. But there's something we've got to get straight. Your uncle Len will be head of the house. We can't have arguments and fallings out. I want you to understand that. Do you understand that?'

''Course,' he said.

'That's all right, then. I'm so pleased. I wanted things sorted out. Funny, en't it? It's like Nan's sorted it out for us.' She started towards the kitchen door then turned and looked back at him. He was messing about with the bike again.

Frank gave the tyre another pumpful of air. As the hissing began he moved it round and marked the spot with some spit. It bubbled. It wasn't as bad as it had seemed. He'd sort it out first thing tomorrow. He glanced towards the kitchen door but Edie had gone inside. So they weren't going back to Swindon, after all. Well, it didn't change anything. It didn't make any difference. His mind was made up.

Chapter 10

Mill had had no word from Dieter since the afternoon when Les had seen them together. And her brother had hardly spoken to her since. Though it was obvious he hadn't said anything to anyone else either. She was grateful for that. But what gave her most pain was trying to imagine what Les must be thinking about her. Because it wasn't true. All she and Dieter did was talk and walk along together. If Les was just to meet him he'd soon see how nice he was. He would, wouldn't he?

She had gone to their meeting place regularly, hoping her friend would be waiting but there had been no sign of him. That worried her. Because he'd said he'd be there. He'd promised. But what worried her more was the possibility of his doing the other thing he'd said he'd do: coming to find her. Surely he wouldn't think of coming to the house?

Her hopes and her anxiety found her time and again standing on the doorstep or out in the Thrales' yard peering down the lane, searching the surrounding fields for any sign of him.

She was at the kitchen door when Les left that morning. She heard Vera call to him. And then she felt him standing behind her. She stepped aside. 'All right, Les?' she said. But he didn't answer.

Vera had come to the door too. 'Take extra care, Leslie,' she called. 'The Germans will be even more nervous than usual after that business with the train.' But Les didn't seem to have heard. 'Mildred, is everything all right?' she asked, as they watched him cross the yard. 'Have you two fallen out?'

Mill so wanted to tell her. Because Vera would know how to explain what was happening. How to make them all friends. She'd know how to do that.

'Nah,' she said. 'You know what he's like sometimes.'

'As long as that's all, dear. One should never let the sun go down on one's anger. Especially when we're angry with those we love. These days we can lose touch with each other so easily.'

'Don't say that, Mrs Thrale.'

'I'm afraid it's the painful truth.'

'Mrs Thrale?'

'Yes?' She saw Mill hesitate. 'Yes, dear?'

'They're not all bad, are they—the Jerries?'

'No, of course not. My parents had several German friends and they were some of the nicest people I've ever met. We must always judge people by what they are, Mildred. Not by their names, or what they say, or what they seem to be, but by what they are.'

'So you could have one for a friend . . . ' said Mill. And added quickly, 'If they were nice?'

'Of course.'

'People don't think so though, do they?'

'Well, I do.' Vera looked at her for a moment. Then: 'Is your friend nice?' she said.

Mill turned away. And Vera saw her nod.

'I'm glad.'

'Mrs Thrale,' said Mill, turning to her desperately, 'you won't tell on me, will you?'

'My dear, as far as I'm aware there's nothing to tell. I trust you, you know that. I don't think you'd ever do anything that you'd be ashamed of.'

''Course not!' said Mill. And blushed. 'He's only a soldier, Mrs Thrale. That's all. And we only talk and walk about together. No one sees us . . . '

'Except Leslie—he's seen you, hasn't he?'

Mill sighed. 'Yes. And now he hates me.'

'And that's what's making him so angry?'

'Yes. And . . . Oh, Mrs Thrale, I haven't seen Dieter for days. He said he'd come and look for me but I haven't seen him. What can I do, Mrs Thrale? And what can I do about Les? I don't know what to do about any of it.'

When he saw the car approaching Les stuck out his thumb and waited. It slithered to a halt further along the icy road and the passenger door swung open.

'Nice day for it,' observed Stan cheerfully as his guide clambered in.

There was only one road along the foot of the Downs and Les's navigational skills weren't strictly necessary. But the lad did know the countryside inside out; and that, the salesman decided, would come in very handy if the worst came to the worst. And it might.

'Haven't got a lot to say for yourself, have you?' he said, after they had driven a mile or two. 'Something on your mind?'

Les shrugged.

'Don't get me wrong; I'm not saying keeping your mouth shut is a bad thing. Especially in this line of business. Still, a bit of conversation helps the journey pass, you know.'

'Are you a real salesman?' said Les.

'As a matter of fact, I am. And a pie-hot one, too.' Crompton laughed. 'Mind you,' he said ruefully, 'it was having such a high opinion of myself put me on that ship to America.'

'America? Have you been to America?'

'Not long before war broke out. Well, life wasn't being what you could call altogether generous so I thought I'd chance my arm in the Land of the Free.'

'What happened?'

'Not a lot. They're all salesmen over there; I just got lost in the crowd. Matter of fact, I was trying to get back to Blighty when the war started. In the end it was the

Yanks themselves who arranged that for me. Once they'd decided to join in, of course. They were on the lookout for people who knew the old country, you see? Couldn't use their own, could they? Well, you'd look a bit silly walking round these lanes in a cowboy hat. They trained me up and here I am.'

'Did you come on a ship?'

'Something like that.'

'That's what I'd like to do!' said Les eagerly. 'Be an agent and that.'

'Would you? It's not everybody's cup of tea, of course. But having been in the selling line I suppose I was suited. I've got the gab, you see? I can do all the chat. And I've always travelled light. Always ready to move on at a minute's notice.'

'And what about . . . what about your family?'

Crompton shook his head. 'No family. Well, not to speak of. Besides, you have to cut yourself off. It gets too complicated otherwise. No ties, you see; that's very important.'

'What about being brave?'

The salesman smiled. 'Steady on, old man.'

'You must be a bit brave cos you're in danger all the time.'

'They reckon a wireless operator lasts three months on average. So there's a week or two in the old dog yet, eh? I try not to think about it. Well, no one fancies getting caught, do they? 'Course, if I was . . . ' Crompton hesitated. 'My employers have been very considerate in that area,' he said. 'I'd be dead before the Nasties could get anything out of me. It's quite painless. Or so it says on the bottle . . . ' He tapped his pocket. And frowned. 'Damn! I've left them on the table again. Ah well! Brave? No, I suppose it's people like the professor I reckon are the brave ones. I mean, he doesn't seem cut out for this lark at all. It must take guts when he does have a go. And you've got to take your hat off to guts. Whoa!' His foot stamped on the brake and he slowed the car to a crawl.

'Now what do they want?' he said. 'Easy does it, Les. Sit tight and let me do the talking.'

The soldiers had been waiting at the roadside where the hill began. The sergeant came towards the car and the other one followed, unslinging his rifle.

Crompton wound down the window. '*Guten tag*,' he said smiling. 'Is there a problem?'

'*Papieren, bitte?* Papers, please.'

It was nice now that Vera knew. A relief. But the trouble was even Vera didn't seem to have an answer to it all.

Mill was beginning to think that it was probably a good thing that Dieter hadn't kept his promise. She couldn't bear to go on waiting and trying to cope with Les being so horrible all the time. Now she'd be able to say to him: Les, I haven't seen him again. You can stop being so angry with me. I ain't seen him. That's what you wanted, wasn't it?

But it wasn't what she wanted. She wanted desperately to see her friend again. And what was wrong with that? She'd give it until . . . until when? Until that big cloud disappeared behind the hill. She'd wait in the lane till then and then she'd go back to Thrales'.

She opened her book and tried to read. It was the one she'd been reading the day she'd first met him, *A Tale of Two Cities*. She didn't seem to have read much of it since then. Not since the day she'd seen him standing over there where the lane turned. Where that soldier had appeared. The one who was all bundled up against the cold. The one who was waving at her. Waving at her? Was he waving to her? He was. And . . . Oh, it was! It was! Wasn't it?

'Dieter?' she called tentatively. Then loudly: 'Dieter! Dieter!'

And he waved again and ran towards her.

His face was pinched and he was shivering. 'Dieter,

you don't half look cold,' she said. And brushed some snow from the shoulder of his greatcoat.

'Millicent, I had almost given up hopes,' he said. 'Because I did not know where to find you.' He smiled. 'I could not knock at everyone's door and ask if Millicent lives here.'

She laughed. 'No,' she said, 'no, I s'pose not. I just thought you must have . . . '

'What?'

'Nothing. I'm ever so pleased to see you, Dieter.'

'I was afraid you would think that I . . . '

'No, I didn't think that,' she said quickly. 'I knew you'd come and find me.'

They stood looking at each other and then at the same moment both looked away.

'You've been working hard, have you?' she asked.

'Yes.' He was silent for a while. And then: 'Millicent?' he said. 'I have been thinking of what we said about the work I do.'

'It don't matter, Dieter; I told you before.'

'It does matter. But what I want to tell you is that the work I do could never harm you. I want you to know this. My work is not a thing that could concern you.'

'That's all right, then.'

'Because I would not want anything to harm you. Because you are . . . Well, you must believe me when I say so, that is all.'

'I do,' she said and felt her face burning. His hand was very light on her arm but she could feel his fingers through the cloth of her coat. ''Course I do!'

'Come,' he said. 'We will walk along together.'

Like spectres. There were four of them standing in the half-light of the musty-smelling crypt. Their faces had been camouflaged with flour and they wore long white sheets which were cowled and covered them from head to toe.

'You were supposed to be here yesterday,' said the bearded leader.

'I couldn't risk it,' said Crompton. 'Not after what happened in Worthing. The roads were full of Jerries.'

'You took a risk coming in the car.'

'It was that or nothing.'

'Where's the boy, the other one?'

'He had a bereavement.'

'You don't sound like a Yank.'

'I'm not a Yank,' said Crompton indignantly.

'And what's he doing with you?'

'This is Les. He knows the countryside.'

The partisan nodded to one of his companions, who produced Crompton's 'samples case' and handed it to the salesman.

'The Worthing group have gone to earth temporarily,' he said. 'But things are warming up. That supply train was just a beginning. Time's short. You and I need to talk, Crompton.' He turned to one of the others. 'Take the boy outside.'

'Oh, why?' pleaded Les. 'That's not fair. Mr Crompton?'

But the salesman shook his head. 'Don't argue, Les.'

Les was taken up the steps and out through the door which was then closed and he and his guard were left sheltering in the porch.

'I thought you was a real Jerry when you stopped us,' said Les.

The cloaked figure did not reply. His attention was concentrated on the road below, as he scanned it constantly in both directions.

'You know, with the accent and everything.'

There was still no answer.

Les persisted. 'You from round here?' he asked. 'Was it your lot who derailed that train?'

Again there was no answer.

'Oh, be fair!' he said. 'Why won't you talk to me?'

'You ask too many questions,' said the partisan.

'Cos I want to know,' said Les. 'What's wrong with that?'

'What you don't know you can't tell, boy. This isn't a game.'

'I know it's not! And you ain't the only one who wants to fight them, you know.'

'You want to fight, do you? Well, you'll get your chance soon enough,' said the partisan. 'The time's coming when we're going to need everyone we can get.'

The door opened and the rest of the group emerged. The leader turned to Crompton who was standing on the stairs below.

'Give us three minutes,' he said, 'and then go back to your car. Understood?'

Crompton nodded. 'Good luck,' he said.

'Luck's got nothing to do with it, friend.'

Les was ushered inside again and the door closed. He turned to Crompton. 'What did he say to you?' he asked.

'Eh? Oh, details. Just details.'

When the three minutes were up they opened the door. There was no sign of the partisans.

'Tough hombres, eh?' said Crompton, as they hurried down the path. 'Enough to give you the creeps with those cloaks and white faces. Like a lot of bloomin' ghosts.'

But they weren't ghosts, thought Les; they were the real thing. They were the ones fighting back. Giving the Jerries what for. Making them pay for . . . for everything.

'Listen,' said Crompton, 'I want to stop at this villa or whatever it is on the way home—the one that old Sims goes on about. Just to have a look at it. Tip us the wink when we're getting near, will you?'

Les nodded.

Both of them seemed pre-occupied on the return journey and they hardly spoke as they drove along. And Patfield almost took Les by surprise.

'This is it!' he said, pointing. 'Stop here.'

Crompton pulled on to the grass verge and turned off the engine. The remains of the villa and its outbuildings lay on either side of the road, on the open field next to the wood and on the slope running up the hill. Many of the walls and floors were still visible; and there were areas where what looked like the cellars had been exposed. But it was hard for an unpractised eye to make any sense of it all—to see the palace in all those fallen stones.

'Doesn't look much, does it?' said Crompton.

'Old Sims thinks so,' said Les.

'He does, doesn't he?' Crompton sighed. 'I'm afraid he's going to take it badly.'

'Take what?' said Les.

Crompton looked across at him. Then he leaned back in his seat and tipped back his hat. 'Do you really want to fight the Nasties, Les?' he said. 'No, just hold on before you answer. I'm talking about the real thing. Not the sort of games I play. I'm talking about life and death.'

'Like the partisans.'

'Yes. Is that what you want to do?'

''Course I do! More than anythin'! I hate the Jerries, Mr Crompton. I want to fight them more than anything.'

'Well, you're going to get your chance.'

'How d'you mean?'

'There's going to be an ambush.'

'An ambush?'

Stan nodded.

'Is that what they told you when I was outside?' said Les.

'It's tomorrow afternoon. There's a small troop convoy coming through and the partisans are going to attack it. They need every man they can find and . . . '

'I'll go! I'll be there!'

'I thought that's what you'd say.'

'Where? Where's it going to be?'

'Not far.' Crompton gestured with his thumb. 'Out there,' he said.

'What d'you mean?'

'I mean Patfield Palace. They reckon it's ideal what with the hill up there and the wood on the other side of the road. They're going to attack them here.'

''Struth!' exclaimed Les. 'I see what you mean about Mr Sims.'

'He's not going to be too pleased, is he?'

'No, he ain't. But I'm on for it, Mr Crompton. Just try and stop me.'

'Oh, I wouldn't do that, Les,' said Crompton and smiled. 'And, look here, I think you ought to call me Stan, don't you?'

'Right ho!'

'That's settled, then.' He turned on the ignition. 'Shevington next stop, eh?' he said. '"Home, James, and don't spare the 'orses!"'

Corporal Mainz made his way down the steps to the military canteen in the basement of Shevington Hall. He was looking forward to some hot coffee before returning to his patrol duties.

As he pushed open the door a colleague from the Communications Room looked up and cupped a hand to his ear: 'Is there anybody there?' he called. The others at the table laughed. But Dieter took no notice. He was happy. He was always happy after his walks with Millicent.

'"Expert" Mainz,' the soldier called, as Dieter approached the counter, 'you are in great demand.'

'Me?'

'Lang was here ten minutes ago. You must go at once to speak to the General.'

As well as the General and Lang there were four other men seated at the table in von Schreier's office. They wore civilian clothes. But there was no mistaking who they were: Gestapo.

'Mainz,' said the General, 'these gentlemen are from the Subversion Unit of the *RSHA*. They have come to help us find our phantom.'

'He is not a phantom, Herr General,' said the civilian who sat nearest von Schreier. 'The inability of your people to find him is evidence only of their limited efficiency, not of his supernatural qualities.'

'What have you to say for yourself, Mainz?' said the General.

Dieter looked round at the faces seated along the table. The one who had spoken so dismissively to the General was turning the pages of a notebook. The other three were looking straight in front of them. 'Herr General . . . '

'Give your evidence to Inspector Reiss, Mainz,' said the General. 'He is the policeman.'

The Inspector looked up from his notes and tapped the map in front of him. 'Corporal, these previous locations go back over a month and more,' he said.

'That was before I arrived, Inspector.'

'And they take place over several counties.'

'That has been the problem. He has always been on the move. I think he is aware of our direction-finding capabilities.'

'An enemy agent would hardly be otherwise, Corporal. But this last transmission, this is very close?'

'Yes, Inspector.'

'Good.' The Inspector smiled. But the smile disappeared as quickly as it had come. 'Then why is it proving so difficult to locate him?'

'His transmissions are infrequent. They are . . . I have . . . working with the truck and one car I have reduced the possible areas in which the transmission took place from triangles with sides of fifteen kilometres to one with sides of five kilometres.'

The Inspector waved the explanation away. He turned to the General. 'We will look into this matter ourselves, Herr General. With the assistance of our vehicles and your tracing-truck there is no reason why we should not be able to reduce the triangle even further. Once that is achieved we will await further transmissions and then employ field-monitors to walk the area that remains. We will snuff out this candle,' he said, and closed the notebook.

Dieter looked across at the General. 'Herr General . . . '

But von Schreier interrupted him: 'Speak to the Inspector, Mainz.'

'Inspector, I need one more transmission,' said Dieter, 'that is all. And if everything is on stand-by, the field-walkers and the rest of it, I guarantee that I can locate this illegal. I request you to allow me one more watch.'

The Inspector did not look up. 'You have until tomorrow morning. Eight o'clock tomorrow morning.'

When Mainz had gone Lang got up and began to pour coffee for the General and his visitors.

Von Schreier sat back in his chair. 'I'm pleased you have allowed him a chance to prove himself,' he said. 'Young Mainz was specially trained for this business. It means a great deal to him.'

The Inspector shrugged. 'It is of no consequence. If he succeeds all well and good,' he said. 'If he fails we will simply proceed as planned.'

'As planned?'

'I intend to search every house within the triangle established by the last transmission.'

'Every house? And you think that will unearth the terrorist?'

'Let us hope so. If not, it will certainly give anyone tempted to aid and support him good reason to reflect. Our searches are very thorough. And now, Herr General, perhaps we might move on to the matter of the convoy?'

The General frowned. 'I would have appreciated more notice of such an event,' he said irritably.

'It has, inevitably, been a matter of the strictest security,' the Inspector replied. 'Given what happened in Worthing.'

'It leaves less than a day to make the necessary arrangements.'

'It leaves less than a day for mistakes to occur, Herr General.'

Les and Stan's journey back to Shevington was uneventful.

Not far from the village they met a patrol-lorry going the other way but the officer sitting next to the driver glanced only briefly at the man and boy in the car and it passed them by.

Stan grinned. 'Won't be long now.'

'I'm hungry,' said Les.

Stan laughed. 'I'm starving! It's fear gives you an appetite. Nearly there.'

And they were. They weren't more than a mile from Shevington when Stan glanced in his rear-mirror and winced. 'Me and my mouth,' he muttered. The patrol-lorry had reappeared. It had turned and was following them. 'We've got company, Les.'

'Are you sure it's us they're after?' said Les.

'Can't risk it,' said Stan. 'Hold tight!' He accelerated gently. But the lorry continued to gain on them. The salesman shook his head: 'It's no good,' he said. 'I can't outrun that thing.'

'We don't have to,' said Les. 'On the left! Turn sharp left when we get round the corner!'

'What?'

For a moment, as they rounded the corner, they lost sight of their pursuers.

'Left! Now!' shouted Les, indicating a narrow gap in the trees. 'Turn now! Turn up the track and keep going!'

Crompton swung the wheel frantically and the car swerved off the road.

'And again!' said Les. 'Left again!'

The car careered to the left bumping along a rutted track that led into the wood, branches clattering on its roof and windows.

'Keep going, Stan!' Les called. Then suddenly: 'Stop here!'

The car skidded to a halt and Crompton hastily switched off the engine.

They held their breath. And heard the lorry roar past on the road beyond. And then everything was silent.

Stan took out a handkerchief and wiped his forehead.

He was sweating. 'That was too bloody close for comfort,' he said.

'Now what?' asked Les.

'We'll have to keep off the road. But it's a fair old haul to carry the radio through the woods to my digs.'

'We'll take it home with me, then,' said Les. 'Thrales' is nearer.'

'With you?'

'You can come and collect the car later. It's well hidden.'

'Keeper Thrale, eh?' Crompton considered for a moment. 'All right.'

It was muddy and treacherous underfoot and the going through the wood was slow. But they made good progress. Until, after half a mile or so, without warning, somewhere to the right of them a dog began to bark. They stopped and looked anxiously towards the trees from which the sound had come. The barking began again, closer now, and was answered by two or three other dogs; and that was followed by the noise of men advancing quickly through the undergrowth.

'*Halt!*' they heard someone shout. 'Halt or we fire! *Hände hoch! Halt!*'

'The Jerries!' said Crompton. 'Run for it, Les! Run!'

They turned and ran. But as they did the salesman stumbled. He fell forward, put out his hands to save himself, and lost his grip on the case which tumbled down the bank into the gully below. He was on all fours in the mud looking down at it as Les came running back to him.

'Stan? Stan, what are you doing?' Then Les saw the case.

'No, leave it,' gasped Crompton. The dogs and shouts were nearer now. 'Leave it and save yourself!'

But Les pushed past him and plunged down the bank. He grabbed the case and was climbing up again when the shot rang out.

Chapter 11

The precise crack of the rifle-shot echoed through the bare trees. And was followed almost at once by another. And another.

Crompton reached down and pulled Les clear of the gully. 'It's me they want,' he said. 'Take the case and run for it. I'll lead them in the other direction.'

'No!' said Les.

'Les, do what you're told!'

'No!' Les grabbed Crompton by the lapel of his coat and pulled him down out of sight. 'It's not us they're after.'

Into the clearing opposite had stumbled George Poole and his father, Harry. Harry Poole was breathing hard. 'I can't,' they heard him say; 'I can't go no further, George.' At once father and son were surrounded by soldiers and dogs. They threw their arms in the air and were bundled away at rifle point.

Les and Stan watched as one of the patrol picked up the bag Harry Poole had dropped. He shook it and out fell a rabbit. His dog pounced on it but the soldier hauled him off. He replaced the rabbit in the bag and slung it over his shoulder. The dog meanwhile had lost interest in the bag; it was pulling hard on its leash and growling in the direction of the undergrowth where Stan and Les were hiding. '*Riechst du noch ein anderes Kaninchen?*' they heard the soldier say. '*Oder was?*' He began to walk forward. But a shout from his companions stopped him; and man and dog turned and set off back the way they had come.

Crompton took out his handkerchief and mopped his brow. 'That was the landlord of the pub and his son, wasn't it?' he said. 'What were they doing here?'

'Thieving,' said Les.

'Well, they're for it now.'

Les stood up. 'Serves 'em right. Come on. Thrales' ain't far.'

When his relief-watch arrived Dieter Mainz sent him away and remained on duty. The 'illegal' would transmit again soon. He must. And when he did, he—Dieter Mainz—and no one else would be listening.

He would show these civilians! These policemen! What were they trained to do? To shout at people. To beat people up. Oh, everyone knew what they were like, these Gestapo fellows. What did they know about the beautiful and complex machinery of unseen voices he had been trained to hear and name? They had no idea. Put them somewhere like . . . Yes, like the Central Control in Berlin! Take them there and they would be completely lost! Berlin Central: that vast room with row after row of operators lit by the watery glow from the screens of three hundred panoramic receivers. Receivers that could isolate and extract the most tenuous Morse from a snowstorm of static. Each skilled operator with his telephone to hand ready to alert Brest, Augsburg, and Nuremberg to any transmission from a frequency outside those known to be under German control. Any transmission whatsoever. There was nothing that could not be found.

Dieter adjusted the volume control and the whistling in his headphones subsided to a monotone whine. With his fingertips he gently, so gently, eased the tuner on and coaxed the needle slowly round the arc of the illuminated dial. The whine rose to a whistle again which became a wail and the wail in its turn was lost in an insistent hiss of static.

It was like listening to an orchestra. Not that the

corporal had listened to many orchestras. But that was how the instructor at the Wehrmacht's Signals School had explained it. 'Like listening to a mighty symphony, gentlemen—in which it is your job to pay attention to only one instrument and to only one player of that instrument!'

And Dieter had been trained to pay attention. To listen. He would know the tune when he heard it. He would show them how it was done.

'I will prove it to you, Millicent!' he said quietly. 'And I will tell you how it was me who showed them how these things are done. And you will be proud of me.'

Alec Thrale was crossing the yard when Les and Stan came hurrying up the lane.

'What was all that carry-on t'other side of the wood?' he called.

'Jerries,' said Les. 'They caught George Poole.'

'George Poole?'

'George and his dad,' said Les. 'They're the ones who've been robbing our traps. Mr Thrale, we need your help.'

'Do you now? We'd better go inside.'

Vera glanced up as they came into the kitchen. 'You look as though you've been running, Leslie,' she said.

'Where's Mill?' asked Les.

'Mildred? She's down in the village. What's that you've got there? And who's this gentleman?'

'It's a wireless. And this is Stan Crompton. And . . . well, you'd better explain, Stan.'

'I don't think he needs to do that,' said Vera. She glanced at Alec. 'What can we do for you, Mr Crompton?'

'I need to see if it's been damaged.'

'Alec?' said Vera. And Thrale nodded.

Les placed the case on the table. Crompton opened it and lifted out the sample-tray. They watched as he slipped the headphones on and released the Morse-key. He was about to commence transmission when the door opened and Mill walked in.

She stared at the man sitting at the table.

'Shut the door, dear,' said Vera calmly. 'This is rather important.'

Crompton adjusted the dial and began to tap out his call sign in the silent kitchen.

Mill could feel her brother's gaze but didn't dare to look back at him.

After only a moment or two Crompton shook his head. 'There's something wrong,' he said and pulled off the headphones. 'I can't get a signal.' He folded the Morse-key away and closed the lid. 'Well, it won't do any harm to shut down for a while till I can see to repairing it. That detector lorry's been a bit too busy lately. Look here, I know it's asking a lot, but I don't think it would be wise for me to take it with me; I don't suppose there's any chance you'd let me leave it here?'

'Of course, Mr Crompton,' said Vera briskly; 'I know just the place. Come along, Mildred.'

'What is it?' said Mill.

'It's a wireless, dear.'

'You don't have to tell everybody!' said Les.

'Don't be silly, Leslie; Mildred isn't "everybody".' She picked up the case and beckoned Mill to follow.

'I'm obliged to you, Mr Thrale,' said Crompton. 'And more than obliged to you, Les. This lad's as good as any man in a tight corner, Mr Thrale. Cool as a blessed cucumber.'

'Sounds like you done well, Leslie,' said Alec.

But Les's thoughts seemed to be elsewhere. He was staring down the passage along which Vera and Mill had disappeared.

'I'd best get back to the car,' said Crompton starting for the door. 'That patrol won't be looking for anyone else now they've got those two. Not for a while anyway.'

He shook hands with Thrale. And then turned to Les. 'Council of War, Les,' he said. 'Find Frank and meet me at Myrtle Lodge pronto. We need a pow-wow.'

Frank felt much better now he'd come to a decision. Though it actually felt more like the decision had come to him. His aunt Edie reckoned Nan had somehow sorted out the Worths' decision about staying on in the cottage. Well, he reckoned Nan had sorted out his decision too.

The decision had been easy. The difficult part would be telling Les; trying to explain it to him. Then again, perhaps Les might even . . . Well, he'd just have to wait and see.

He waited at the oak for over an hour, knowing that this was the road Crompton and Les would return by. But they seemed to be much later than Crompton had said they'd be. And Frank was relieved when he finally saw his friend come running along the road from the direction of Thrales'.

'Les?' he called. 'Is everything all right? Was there trouble?'

And Les breathlessly told him. How he and Stan had given the Nasties the slip. They wasn't more'n six feet away, Frank! And what had happened to the Pooles. Thievin' perishers! They got what they deserved.

'And what about the wireless?'

The wireless? The wireless was on the blink.

'So what's happened to it?'

It was at Thrales'. And that's all Les seemed to want to say about it.

'What, you mean hidden?' Frank asked.

Yes. No—he didn't know where. Didn't want to know. Vera knew. And Mill.

'But, listen, Frank, there's news. The partisans . . . '

But Frank had news of his own. And it wouldn't

wait. 'Les?' he said. 'Les, you remember what Nan said?'

'What? You mean about lookin' out for each other?'

'About never giving up.'

'Yes, 'course. "Consider Garibaldi!" That's what she used to say, wasn't it?'

'Yes. I've been thinking about that, Les.'

'What about it?'

'That's what I've got to do.'

'How d'you mean?'

'That's why I'm leaving.'

'Leaving Nan's?'

'Yes. I've made up my mind.'

Les nodded. 'Fair enough,' he said. 'D'you want me to ask Alec and Vera to find you somewhere with us?'

'With you?'

'Yeah. We've got room. They won't mind. I'll ask 'em, shall I?'

'No,' said Frank. This was harder than he'd thought. 'No, don't do that, Les. Look . . . ' He hesitated.

'Look what?'

'It's not just Nan's, Les.'

'What ain't?'

'It's Shevington; I'm leaving Shevington.'

'Do what?'

'I'm going to look for my dad. I'm going to try and find him.'

Les shook his head. What was Frank talking about? He couldn't do that.

'No,' he said. 'No, Frank, you can't. Not now. I mean . . . You can't do that.'

'I've got to, Les.'

'No you ain't. You don't understand. There's things we've got to do.'

'Les, I've got to try and find him. I'd given up believing it was true; really believing he was still alive. But Nan never gave up. Ever. And she was right. So I'm going to go and look for him. I've worked it out. I'm going to find out where they're building those roads. Like the one where he wrote the letter from.'

'But, Frank . . . What about Stan and everything? What about fighting the Jerries?'

'This is important, Les.'

'That's important and all!'

'I know. But I can't. I'm going soon. I've got to. Don't you see?'

What was the matter with Les? Why wouldn't he understand? He had to. Because if he didn't then there wasn't much chance of him agreeing to what Frank was going to ask him, was there?

'You do, don't you? Understand?'

And Les nodded.

'You do, don't you! I knew you would!'

Yes, Les understood. He understood all right. First Mill and then Frank. First his sister and now his best friend. There wasn't anyone who wouldn't let you down—not when it came to it—not in the end.

'So what do you think?'

Les shrugged. 'It's up to you, ennit? He's your dad.'

'Yes, I know but . . . You and me, we . . . fact is, Les, I wondered if . . . '

'Look, Frank, I've got to get a shift on, all right? I'm in a hurry. I'll see you later.'

'Les?'

But Les had walked past him; and was already making off down the lane.

'Les? Hold on!'

'There's something I've got to do,' Frank heard him call. And saw his friend raise his hand in what looked like a wave. But he didn't look back.

They were in Crompton's room this time. Stan sat on the bed and Les and Sims on chairs facing him. Stan looked at his watch.

'Shall we wait a bit longer?' he said.

'I told you, Stan,' said Les, 'he ain't coming. Frank don't want anything to do with it any more.'

'Well, I must say I'm very surprised.'

'You did explain to him? About this meeting?' said Sims.

'He ain't interested, Mr Sims. He's got other fish to fry.'

'It's grief,' said Crompton, 'that's what it is. His grandmother being taken so suddenly has hit him hard. Though I never thought he'd just push off like this.'

'Well he has.'

'We'd better get on with it, then. Now, listen, Sims old man, I've got news to tell you. And there may be decisions you'll want to make when you hear what I've got to say. Important decisions.'

'It's a Council of War,' said Les.

'All right, Les; leave it to me. The fact is, old man, tomorrow afternoon there's a troop convoy, a small one, three or four trucks, going east from here. It will pass through Shevington and out along the Middelbury Road. The partisans have been ordered to attack it.'

'Good Lord!'

'It's an ambush!' said Les.

'They haven't got the men to engage the Nasties for any length of time so the idea is to hit them and run.'

'Attack them in Shevington?' said Sims.

'No.' Crompton shook his head. 'Not Shevington.'

'Nearer the coast?'

'No.'

'Where?'

Stan took a deep breath. 'Patfield Palace,' he said.

'Patfield Palace?'

'That's right. They've warned me about it so that I can make shift. You know, clear out and take the wireless to safety.'

'I'm going to fight 'longside them,' said Les.

'But you can't,' said Sims. And they turned to look at

him. 'Not Patfield. No, really. Patfield's . . . You can't conduct a battle on that site.'

'That's the decision they've made,' said Crompton. 'And I've made mine: I'm staying put. It was the wireless brought me here and that's got to be my priority. Besides, it'd be a bit of a giveaway to cut and run. The point is, what are you going to do, old man?'

'But Patfield . . . ' said Sims.

'I can tell you now, the partisans need all the help they can get. Nobody's obliged to volunteer, of course.'

'Come on, Mr Sims,' said Les. 'Side by side. Like it was before, eh?'

'No, Gill. Much as I'd like to join you. This isn't like it was before, don't you see?' Peter Sims ran his hand through his hair. 'I'm afraid this has taken me off guard. I'm . . . I don't know what I am, to be honest. Oh, I don't expect you to understand,' he said. 'Why should you? But the villa . . . Patfield's been an absolutely crucial part of my life.'

'All the more reason to go. There can't be anybody knows that place better than you.'

'I wish that's all there was to it,' said Sims quietly. 'No. This is something I'm going to have to consider very thoroughly. Excuse me.'

He went out and the door closed behind him.

Crompton shook his head. 'I said it would hit him hard, didn't I?'

'He ain't going to fight, is he?'

'I don't reckon he is. Which makes it more of a pity about Frank. Looks like it'll be just you, Les.'

Les ran. And when he got to the Thrales' yard he went straight to the shed where he knew Alec would be.

'Mr Thrale?' he said, bursting in at the door.

The keeper looked up from his chair. 'Leslie?'

'It was me, Mr Thrale,' he said. 'It was me and Frank and Mr Sims, we helped Ted Naylor.'

Thrale took the pipe from his mouth. 'Did you now?'

'Yes. And I'm going to do it again. Fight, I mean. I've got to. They're going to attack a convoy.'

'Hold your horses; you're leaving me behind.'

'They've been ordered to. Out at Patfield tomorrow afternoon.'

'Should you be telling me all this?'

'I trust you, Mr Thrale.' Les sat down suddenly on the box opposite the keeper. 'You're the one I trust.'

'Trust or not, Leslie . . . '

'They need men, Mr Thrale. That's why I'm telling you. We could go together. Will you come?'

The keeper did not reply at once. Les watched him knock the ashes from his pipe.

'Will you, Mr Thrale?'

But Alec shook his head. 'No,' he said; 'no, I don't think I can do that.'

'But, Mr Thrale, why not?'

'I don't say the prospect's not a tempting one.'

'Then why won't you come?'

'Because there's no knowing where that might lead to. And my place is here.' Thrale held up his hand. 'No, just listen to me for a minute. My place is here with Vera and Mill and this house. And there en't no choice in the matter. You see, Leslie, if folk think these times are hard then they ain't give a thought to what's to come. I've given it a deal of thought sitting here these last months. There's times coming as'll take the measure of us even more than them we've been through up to now. When those times come I have to be here for Vera and Mill. That's how I see things. But you're a grown man. Before your time but that's what times have done to you. And you must make your own decisions.'

'I wanted us to fight side by side, Mr Thrale.'

'And I'd be proud to do so.' Like last time, thought the keeper—though I never knew it and you didn't neither, boy. It was true. Les and his friends may have delivered the machinery for Ted's bomb but it was Alec who'd provided the explosives to arm it. Plastic explosive given to him not long before the outbreak of war by a man he'd met by chance—well, it had seemed like chance—at his gunsmith's. A man recruiting men into a Secret Army to lie in wait ready to harry the invader. An army so secret even Vera never knew he was part of it. She still didn't. An army that might yet be called upon to act. Was that what he believed? Alec wondered. Was that what he was waiting for? And decided that yes, that was part of it. And that it was a secret he still could not share. No, not even with this boy who needed all the help and encouragement there was. Deserved it, too.

'Mr Thrale! You're the true article. I know you are.'

Thrale looked back at the boy. Lord, what he'd have given to say yes!

'Come and help us, Mr Thrale? They can be beat. What's happened in Russia shows that, don't it? It do, don't it!'

'Perhaps it do,' said the keeper. 'By God, I hope it do! But that makes no difference to what I've said.'

Les stood up. 'I'm still going, Mr Thrale. I've got to.'

'You must do what you think right, Leslie. Whatever the consequences.'

'Consequences?'

'There'll be consequences, you can rely on that. What does Mildred say about your going?'

'Nothing,' said Les quickly.

'Nothing?'

'I haven't told her.'

Thrale frowned. 'Why not?'

'It's none of her business.'

'You're her business, Leslie; you're her brother.'

'I ain't a kid. You said so yourself. It's up to me what I do. You won't tell her, will you? And Mrs Thrale, I don't want you to tell her neither.'

'If that's what you want.'

'I do.'

'And, Leslie?'

'What?'

'You give some more thought to talking to Mildred, will you?'

Frank had the bike upside down and was replacing the brake-blocks with the new ones he'd found in Nan's repair-kit. He turned the pedal and set the wheel spinning then jammed on the brake-handle. The frame and spokes juddered as the wheel stopped abruptly. Perfect. With the puncture repaired and the brakes renewed the bike was in good nick. It would have to be, he thought; there was no knowing how far it was going to have to carry him.

Had he really thought that Les might come with him? Had he? After all, why should he? It wasn't his dad. Besides, Les had a life of his own. And there was Mill, of course. He couldn't leave Mill. Not just like that. But Frank had no one like that. Not now Nan had gone. No, he'd made the right decision. And the sooner he was on his way the better.

Still, Les had been a bit . . . Frank spun the wheel angrily. Yes, he had! He'd been a bit couldn't-care-less about it, hadn't he. He hadn't expected that from his best friend.

He looked up as he heard the back door open and saw Len Worth come out. Len stepped into the yard and stood for a moment looking up at the holes where the roof-tiles were missing. Then he went back inside.

Len was making himself at home. Well, let him. It was his home now.

Chapter 12

Mill was at the village shop early that morning; but there was already a queue outside the door.

The day was overcast. And the snow had returned. When Mr Dearman finally came to open up she was glad to get inside.

She waited with the other women among the smells of paraffin and damp clothing while the shopkeeper tried to find something on their shopping-lists from his increasingly empty shelves. She was taking out her book when a commotion at the shop door made her look round. Someone was being helped inside. It was Mrs Newton. Mrs Newton was a widow who lived alone on the other side of the church. She was being supported by Mrs Prout and another woman. The queue parted to let them through and they sat her down on a chair. Mrs Newton was out of breath and she had been crying.

'Oh, the wicked devils!' she said.

Then everyone spoke at once. 'Mrs Newton, whatever is it?'

'What's happened, my dear?'

'Has there been an accident?'

'Give her a glass of water.'

'The wicked, wicked devils,' Mrs Newton kept repeating.

Mr Dearman passed over the glass of water and since Mill was nearest she took it and held it while the distraught woman sipped it unsteadily.

'What have they done to you, Mrs Newton?'

'I was never so frightened in all my life.'

'Calm down, Mrs N. You're safe now,' said Mr Dearman.

'To come into a body's house like that.'

'Who was it?' said Mrs Prout.

'Them bloody Germans. God forgive me, I shouldn't use bad language, I know, but I'm so upset. I'm a woman on my own. I en't got no one to look out for me. I ran all the way here.'

'And you're safe now, dear,' said Mrs Prout. 'Take your time and tell us what they wanted. You're safe here.'

'There's nobody safe, Mrs Prout. They're going from house to house.'

'Whatever for?'

'They turned my cottage inside out. I don't know if I shall ever be able to put it all back together properly. All my treasures. They ain't much but they mean a lot to me.'

'Didn't they tell you why? Didn't they give you an explanation?'

'No chance of that,' said one woman. 'They never tell you anything.'

'Except when they're telling you what to do,' said another.

'What do they think I am?' said Mrs Newton. 'What would I be doing with a blessed wireless?'

'A wireless?'

'Or somesuch thing. I don't know. Whatever it was they didn't have cause to go and do that to my home. There's no call to treat people like that. It's just wickedness.'

'For a blessed wireless? Well, if that don't put the tin lid on it! Wickedness is just what it is! Right!' said Mrs Prout. 'We're going next door to The Office and lodge a complaint.'

'Oh, Mrs Prout, no!' said Mrs Newton. 'Don't do that. I don't want to make a fuss.'

'That's the very thing we've got to do. And it's about time we damned well did. Straws and camels' backs, Mrs

Newton. If that's the sort of trick they've started playing then nobody's safe from them. Who's coming with me next door to tell them what we think?'

There was a murmur of agreement. 'Come on, then,' said Mrs Prout; and turned to Mill. 'What about you, young woman?'

'Me?'

'Are you coming with us?'

'I can't,' said Mill anxiously. 'I can't; I've got to get home.'

'Well, Mainz?' said Lang, who had chosen not to ride with the Gestapo men. 'Our friends from the *RSHA* seem very good at ransacking houses but rather less efficient when it comes to finding enemy agents.'

'If they had given me more time I could have located him precisely and there would be no need for this, Oberleutnant. I am trained to operate wirelesses not to search people's homes.'

'I'm enjoying this no more than you are,' said Lang; 'but the General insists that we are present. Tell me, Mainz, confidentially, I assume this triangle you've drawn is accurate?'

'Absolutely precise, Oberleutnant,' replied Mainz indignantly. 'The illegal is somewhere here. I am certain of it.'

'I hope so, Mainz. For your sake.'

The tracking-truck lurched to a stop. And Lang pulled aside the canvas and looked out. For some reason they had drawn up outside the *BKVZ* and their driver was getting down and going round to open the bonnet.

The dark Mercedes leading the search party stopped too and Inspector Reiss jumped out and ran back to the truck.

'*Was gibt's?*' he demanded.

'*Es dauert nur einen Augenblick, Inspektor, nicht mehr,*' replied the driver.

'*Selbst für Augenblicke haben wir keine Zeit. Mach'schnell!*'

The Inspector was about to get back into his car when the door of the village shop opened and Mrs Prout and several other women spilled out on to the pavement.

'Is that them?' she demanded. 'Are they the ones?'

Mrs Newton nodded reluctantly. 'I think so.'

'You damned hooligans! Yes, you!' said Mrs Prout, pointing at the Inspector. 'You'll be called to account one of these days if there's any justice. Frightening women and shooting children. That's all you're damn well good for. Well you don't frighten me!'

The sentry outside The Office unslung his rifle as the women advanced on the policeman but hesitated to come forward. The crowd formed a semi-circle in front of Reiss and they all began talking at once.

Dieter Mainz walked to the back of the truck to see what was happening.

Which was when Mill saw him. And, without thinking, she smiled and went to wave.

Which was when he saw her. And saw her smile fade and the look of bewilderment which replaced it. He saw the bewilderment change to horror. And then he looked down at the scene on the pavement below and realized what it was she was seeing.

Mill couldn't take her eyes from the figure on the back of the truck. It was her Dieter! She saw his lips moving. And saw him shake his head. She saw him raise his hand in a desperate gesture of denial.

Millicent? He wanted to call to her. To shout: Millicent, this is not what it seems. I am not part of this.

The driver slammed the bonnet of the truck and climbed back into his cab. The Inspector walked quickly to his car. And the search party swept away along the road leaving Mrs Prout and the others shouting and shaking their fists.

Mill stared after them until the last truck turned the corner. Then she hurried away. And when she knew she was out of sight—she ran.

Muffled in his scarf and overcoat Stan Crompton had drawn his chair close to the makeshift fire that spluttered in his hearth.

There was no question of being out on the road. It would be one of those endless days when the only thing to do was wait. And while he waited he was reading. *The Sidewinder*. There were, of course, one or two pages with which he was already familiar, and one or two paragraphs on those pages which he knew by heart. But despite that it was turning out to be a rattling good yarn. Just the thing for a day like today.

However, as the morning wore on, Stan found himself thinking more and more about old Sims and what had been said at their meeting yesterday; and the fact that he hadn't seen the professor since.

He put down the book, walked along the landing and tapped at his neighbour's door. There was no reply. He tapped again harder and heard Sims call.

'Who . . . Who is it?'

'It's me, old man.' Crompton turned the handle and opened the door. 'Good Lord!' he said.

Peter Sims was wearing a striped college scarf, a trench coat, heavy tweed trousers, and stout walking boots. An ashwood walking stick and a battered trilby hat lay on the chair beside him.

'Hello, Crompton,' he said. 'I was going to pop in and see you.'

Crompton laughed. 'Well, there was no need to dress up, old man—I'm only across the landing.'

'Oh, the togs?' said Sims. 'No, they're my walking clothes.'

The two men stood looking at each other. 'You've made your decision then?' said Crompton.

Sims ran his hand through his hair. 'Yes; it seems I have, doesn't it.'

'Stout man. If I had a hat on I'd take it off to you.'

'Good Lord, there's no need for that. To be honest, it wasn't terribly difficult. Things often aren't as difficult as one imagines, are they? You see, it struck me that there can be no better use for the Past than to put it to the service of the Future. Oh, dear. That probably sounds rather pompous to you. But the fact is I've spent so much of my life living in the Past,' Sims gestured to the shelves, 'surrounded by it actually, I seem to have lost sight of so much else. I'm not brave, you see, but I'd forgotten the enormous satisfaction I got from trying to be. Sitting here last night it struck me that it was time I did something about it. I feel quite relieved. Is something wrong?'

'What? No, I don't think so,' said Crompton, looking round the room. What was it? There was something odd about it. Something he couldn't quite put his finger on.

He watched Sims gather his hat and stick from the chair. 'But are you sure you're all right, old man?' he said. 'You look a bit pale.'

'I didn't get much sleep, that's all it is,' said Sims. 'As a matter of fact, I feel rather . . . rather fit! Yes, indeed. And a bit of a walk will buck me up in no time! After you, Crompton.'

Peter Sims closed the door behind him and started for the top of the stairs. When he was halfway down Ilkley came bouncing along the hall followed by the Misses Elliott, who, when they saw their guest, applauded enthusiastically.

'Oh, how splendid you look, Mr Sims!'

'He so reminds one of dear Leslie Howard, don't you think, Agnes—the film actor?'

'He does! Mr Sims you look positively dashing.'

'Thank you, ladies.'

'Will you be long?'

'That rather depends, you know.'

'Do come in for a pot of tea when you return.'

'I'd like that,' he said. 'You're very kind. Always very kind.' He looked up and called to where Crompton stood at the top of the stairs. '*Ave atque vale*, old man!'

Crompton grinned. 'All the best!'

Sims lifted his trilby in salute. Then he stepped out into the snow.

The ladies returned to their sitting room and Crompton walked back along the landing. He laughed. Fancy the professor turning out to be such a card! It just showed: you never knew people as well as you thought you did. It was all wonderfully odd. And there'd been something odd about his room, too—hadn't there? He pushed open Sims's door and looked inside. The shelves of books were unchanged, the photographs of his university pals on the wall, the table strewn with . . . The table wasn't strewn with anything! The photographs of the villa, the maps and papers had gone; and in their place was a large brown envelope. And written on it in Sims's neat hand were the words: '*For the attention of Mr and Mrs Underwood.*'

It was Rose's room now. She'd hung her best dress from the picture rail; and draped a colourful scarf over the lampshade; and one or two of her film-star postcards were stuck in the frame of the mirror. But on the wall above the bed the man with the beard and blood-red shirt still stared into the sun. Frank was glad about that.

'Frank?'

He turned. She was standing in the doorway watching him.

'Sorry, Rose,' he said. 'I just wanted to look.'

'That's all right,' she said. And saw the case beside him on the floor. She closed the door. 'Frank, what's up?'

'Nothing,' he said. 'I'm glad you've kept Garibaldi.'

'Is that who it is? Well, he looks like a proper hero, doesn't he?'

'That's what Nan used to say.'

'You're going away, aren't you?' she said quietly. 'Frank?'

He nodded.

'You don't have to, you know.'

'I do, Rose. With Nan gone and . . . and everything else.'

'Frank, you don't. Dad can't help himself. He's been through terrible things. But he'll get better; I know he will.'

'It's not that, Rose; I'm going to look for my dad.'

'Your dad? Frank, d'you think he's still . . . '

'Yes! And I'm going to find him. I'm going to find where the Jerries are building roads. That's where I'm going to start. That's where the letter said he was.'

'On your own?'

He nodded.

'What about Les?' she said. 'You two are inseparable. En't he going with you?'

Frank shrugged: 'It's not his dad, is it?'

'When're you going?'

'Now.'

'Frank!'

'While they're all out,' he said. 'It's easier that way. I'm taking the bike.'

'Oh, Frank, I wish you didn't have to go. I wanted you to be here when . . . Frank, I haven't told another soul. Not ma nor anybody. Frank, guess what? Phil Gingell's asked me to marry him!'

' 'Struth!'

'You don't have to sound so surprised,' she said and laughed.

'I'm not. I mean . . . Honest, Rose, I reckon anyone would want to marry you.'

'So next time I see you . . . you know, when you come back . . . you will come back, won't you?'

'I don't know.'

'Oh, Frank, don't say that.'

'Look, tell Colin I said cheerio, eh? And your mum. I

know she tried to make things all right . . . but . . . but . . . well, you know what I mean. I tried, too . . . but . . . '

Rose nodded. 'It's all buts, en't it?' she said. 'That's what's so sad about everything. You will remember me, won't you?'

' 'Course I will. And I hope you do get married, Rose.'

She smiled. 'I might be able to tell them now things have settled down a bit, eh? Oh, Frank, I shall miss you. I will, you know. Go on,' she said; 'go on or I shall cry.'

'Goodbye, Rose.'

And picking up his case he hurried out of the room.

'What's the time, Mr Thrale?'

'About a minute later than the last time you asked me, Leslie,' the keeper replied.

Les nodded.

'Aren't you hungry, Leslie?' said Vera. He had hardly touched his food.

'Not much, Mrs Thrale.'

'I hope you're not sickening for something,' she said.

What was the matter with everyone? Alec was like a bear with a sore head. And Leslie and Mildred still seemed to be at daggers drawn. At least, Leslie did. Mildred just seemed to be on edge. She'd come back from the shop with an empty basket. She'd completely forgotten why she'd gone, she'd said. And she'd hardly said a word since. Vera sighed. The meals the four of them took together in the big, old kitchen were so important. Meals together were occasions of celebration no matter how meagre or plain the fare. But this thoroughly unpleasant atmosphere reminded her of the awful meals her parents and their friends used to share, not long before the end, before their Utopian community fell apart so catastrophically. They'd had such noble aspirations when they'd upped sticks and moved down to Sussex. But it had been a pipe-dream. None of it had been real in any . . . well, in any real sense of the word.

But this little household, her household, was real. And she was jiggered if she was going to let it fall apart. No, it was time to call everyone to order.

'Listen, all of you . . . ' she began.

'Mr Thrale . . . ' said Les.

And Mill snapped. She slammed down her knife and fork. 'Les!' she screamed. 'Les, stop it! What does it matter what time it is? Just shut up about the time.'

Les glared at her across the table. 'Don't tell me what to do,' he said. 'You ain't got no right to tell anyone what to do.'

'Leslie! Be quiet!'

Les looked up. Vera had jumped to her feet. But she wasn't looking at him. She was looking out of the window.

'Alec,' she said. 'Visitors.'

There was a crash as the tailboard of the troop-carrier was let down followed by the sound of boots clattering across the yard. A soldier's face appeared at the window. Then there was a loud knocking at the door.

'I'll deal with this, Vera,' said Alec. 'Sit down all of you.'

The door was thrown open and standing on the step were two civilians.

'Reiss. Gestapo,' said the taller of them. And pushed the keeper aside.

Vera's fingers tightened on the back of the chair. 'What's the meaning of this?' she enquired evenly.

'The meaning of this is that we have reason to believe there have been illegal transmissions made from this house,' replied the Inspector. He stood aside and gestured to the search party waiting outside the door. '*Wir müssen dieser Rundfunk finden. Suchen Sie es überall!*'

The soldiers came in and under the direction of the other Gestapo agents they began to spread out through the house.

Les pushed back his chair and rose slowly to his feet.

He was staring across the table at Mill. His eyes were bright with anger. Or it might have been tears.

'Les . . . ' she said. 'Les, don't look like that . . . ' She turned away from his accusing gaze. And as she did, her hands went up to her face.

In the doorway, standing beside the young army officer, was Dieter. Her Dieter.

And he stared back at her in disbelief. No—it couldn't be? That was too unfair. Not . . . But it was. It was Millicent.

'Les!' she said, turning back to Les. And seeing his look of horror she knew at once what he must be thinking. 'No, Les,' she said desperately. 'I never!'

'You bloody Nasty!' Les hurled himself across the room and the corporal fell to the floor under his hail of blows. Inspector Reiss grabbed Les and began to haul him clear. But Les wasn't going to be taken easily. As soon as he was on his feet he swung a kick at the Gestapo agent which sent him reeling and then he sprinted for the door.

The two soldiers on guard outside were taken by surprise and Les was across the yard and making for the fields before they could throw their weapons to their shoulders. Alec Thrale knocked one of them aside but the second soldier felled him with a blow from his rifle-butt.

Vera screamed: 'Alec!' But Reiss had recovered himself and grabbed her before she could reach her husband. He drew a pistol from his coat.

'*Verfolgen Sie den Jungen!*' he ordered. One of the soldiers ran off in the direction Les had taken. The other one dragged Alec to his feet. There was blood on his cheek and a dark gash under his eye.

'We seem to have stirred the pot,' said the Inspector. And turned to Mainz. '*Vielleicht haben Sie diesmal recht, mein Korporal.*'

Dieter Mainz did not reply. What did it matter if he was right? All he knew was that he had brought them to her door. But how could he have known it was hers?

Millicent? But she had collapsed into her chair and was sitting with her head in her hands. She wouldn't even look at him.

'*Inspektor? Herein!*'

The call came from the Gestapo agent who appeared in the hallway. He was pointing to Vera's room.

The Inspector gestured with his pistol and Alec, Vera, and Mill were herded along the hall and into the room. Lang and Werner followed.

The room was a shambles. Vera's modelling board had been overturned and the shelves had been swept clear and their contents scattered all over the floor. The Gestapo agent was kneeling in front of the fireplace. He looked up as they all appeared in the doorway.

'*Hier gibt's was, Inspektor,*' he said, tapping the brickwork.

'You have something to hide, Frau Thrale?' said the Inspector.

Vera's face registered nothing at all. She took out a handkerchief and gently wiped the blood from her husband's cheek.

'Well, we shall see,' said the Inspector. '*Mach'schnell, Roder!*'

One by one the bricks were removed and thrown into the hearth.

'*Es ist hohl!*' the agent announced triumphantly. '*Da ist ein grosses Loch darin.*'

'*Reichen Sie hinein!*'

Vera placed an arm around Mill's shoulders as they watched the agent direct the light of his torch into the cavity.

'*So?*' demanded the Inspector

The agent frowned. '*Ich sehe nichts.*'

The Inspector pushed him aside. '*Geben Sie mir die Taschenlampe,*' he said. He took the torch and shone the light into the hole. They saw him frown. Then reach inside. When he withdrew his hand he was holding the jewel-case with the worn velvet cover.

'What is this?' he demanded.

'It belongs to me,' said Vera, her voice was unsteady.

The Inspector snapped it open and removed the necklace.

'Why is it hidden?'

'It's a family heirloom,' said Vera. 'It was hidden to keep it out of the hands of thieves.'

The Inspector lifted his hand and seemed about to strike her.

'Frau Thrale,' said Lang quickly. 'The soldiers of Germany, even its policemen, are not thieves. Your necklace is of no interest to us. Isn't that so, Inspector?'

The Inspector snapped the jewel-box shut and tossed it and the necklace aside. 'No interest whatsoever,' he said.

The third Gestapo man appeared in the doorway. '*Wir haben das Haus von oben bis unten durchgesucht*,' he announced. '*Hier ist nichts, Inspektor.*'

The Inspector looked across at Vera. 'You will be pleased to learn, Frau Thrale,' he said, 'that nothing has been found.' And then he turned to Dieter. 'Nothing, Mainz,' he said. 'Yet again. Despite all your diagrams and your expert knowledge. What have you to say?'

Dieter was watching Millicent. Her fingers were pressed tightly over her eyes shutting everything out. But the tears ran between them and down her cheeks. 'I am . . . I am sorry,' he said quietly.

'What did you say, Mainz?'

Dieter turned to meet the policeman's angry gaze. 'I made a mistake,' he said. 'The fault is mine, Inspector.'

'As will be the consequences.'

'*Inspektor? Der Junge . . .* ' called the soldier who ran in from the yard. '*Der Junge ist weg, Inspektor!*'

'*Dummkopf!*' Reiss pushed him aside and strode from the room.

Werner Lang picked up the necklace and its box and handed them to Vera. 'My apologies,' he said, 'for the inconvenience you have suffered. By the way—the boy has escaped.'

'Thank you,' she said. 'Thank you for telling us.'

Lang saluted. And turned to go. He hesitated when he reached the door. Mainz was leaning against the table staring at the weeping girl who sat opposite.

'*Mainz?*'

But the young soldier did not move.

'*Korporal Mainz,*' he said sharply, '*folgen Sie mir!*'

And Dieter Mainz stood up and followed his officer out into the yard.

Vera reached for her husband's arm. 'Sit down,' she said, 'and let me look at that cut.' But Thrale shook his head and remained at the window watching the soldiers as they climbed back aboard the trucks. Vera came and stood beside him. 'It was there, Alec,' she said quietly. 'The wireless was there. I can't think what's become of it.'

They turned to see Mill rush out along the passage and through the kitchen.

The tracking-truck was starting out of the yard and Dieter stood under the canvas looking back at the house. As he saw her emerge he couldn't stop himself, he called to her: 'Millicent?' But it was no use, she was looking in the other direction. And then the lorry turned the corner and she was lost to sight.

'Les? Les?' she was calling.

'Comfort her, Vera,' said Thrale.

Vera hurried to where Mill was kneeling. She put an arm around her shoulders. 'He got away, dear. That's the important thing. Leslie knows these woods inside out. He'll be safe enough until we can . . . Alec?' she said anxiously, as her husband walked past. 'Alec, where are you going?'

'To look for Leslie.'

'But where?'

'I think I know where to find him.'

Chapter 13

He had no idea when the ambush was to take place, or the slightest inkling of how these things were managed. When he emerged from the trees Peter Sims found Patfield Palace deserted.

He stood at the edge of the wood looking fondly at the ruins. By the end of the day, even the poor shadow that remained of Patfield's glory might exist no longer.

The falling snow had concealed the site beneath a smooth white blanket. But Peter Sims knew those mounds and gullies like the back of his hand, better; and, like a magician, he could raise the villa's painted walls and tiled courtyards at a glance. Glorious Patfield! Henry Underwood had been right to believe it was a palace. It was. Because one needed to believe in palaces. That was what he had decided, sitting in the early hours with his notebooks and maps and Henry's photographs all round him. Yes—and one needed to look for them. That was the important thing. It was the conclusion which filled the final page of the Patfield manuscript which he had left on his table for Henry's parents.

A movement where the road turned made him look up. The figure cycling purposefully along seemed familiar.

'Tate?' he called.

'Mr Sims?' Frank rode up quickly and pulled in beside the teacher. 'I didn't realize it was you,' he said.

Sims smiled. 'Dressed for the occasion, you know, Tate. But what are you doing here?'

'I'm leaving, Mr Sims. I'm going to look for my dad.'

'Your father? Ah, I see. Yes, that explains it. Gill

didn't make that clear. Well, I can think of few better reasons. And, of course, I wish you well. I hope you find him. Though I'm sorry you're not going to be with us.'

'With you what, sir?'

'In the ambush, Tate.'

'The ambush?'

'Though I do understand that finding your father has to take priority.'

'Mr Sims, I don't know nothing about any ambush.'

Sims frowned. 'But Crompton brought the news yesterday afternoon. That's why I'm here. The partisans are going to ambush a convoy and they need help.'

'Here?'

'Yes.'

'Mr Sims, I didn't know anything about it.'

'But Gill told us . . . Gill was quite sure . . . he said you'd want no part of it.'

'Les said that?' said Frank. 'Mr Sims, it's not true. How could you think I . . . 'Course I do!'

'Do you? Do you? Oh, how splendid! This is such good news.' Sims held out his hand. 'It'll be like old times,' he said. And Frank could have sworn the teacher blushed.

'But why did Les say a thing like that?'

'I've no idea.'

'Is he supposed to be here?'

'Oh, yes! I'm surprised he's not here already. He was most eager.'

'What are we supposed to do?'

'That I don't know. Wait, I imagine. Until something happens.'

They didn't have to wait long. Soon after they had withdrawn into the trees there was movement on the hillside opposite. A file of half a dozen men wearing white hooded cloaks made their way slowly down to the road. Two of them carried what looked like a machine-gun.

'We'd best make ourselves known,' said Sims. And he and Frank walked from the trees.

The cloaked figures raised their weapons.

'It's all right,' shouted Frank. 'It's me. The one who brought the wireless.'

'Why don't you just wave a damned great flag,' said the bearded leader angrily. 'What the hell are you doing here?'

'Mr Crompton told us that you needed help,' said Sims.

'Oh, he did, did he? Give them a sheet to cover themselves, for God's sake. We might as well write our names in the snow otherwise. Can either of you use a gun?' he demanded.

'I'm afraid not,' said Sims. And Frank shook his head.

'You're not a lot of use, are you?'

'I've got the bike,' said Frank.

'What about you?'

'I do know the villa rather well,' said Sims.

'You what?'

'I thought it might be of some help. I've been studying . . . '

'For God's sake, man, we're not a bloody archaeological society. And you can't use a gun?'

'No.'

'You may have to learn before the afternoon's over. Meanwhile just keep out of our way and out of sight. I want us in place quickly so the snow will cover our tracks.'

Frank and Sims took the white cloaks they were handed and slipped them over their heads.

'Right,' said the partisan. 'Now go where you're told to go. And take that damned bicycle with you. Move!'

His men began to disperse about the ruins: in the wood and behind the wall on the hill above. But as they took up their positions another figure appeared, hurrying through the snow.

'It's Mr Thrale!' said Frank.

'Who?'

'Mr Thrale's all right.'

'He's a dead man if he's not,' muttered the bearded leader, taking the pistol from his belt.

'Frank?' Thrale called. 'Frank, is that you? Is Leslie with you?'

'No,' replied Frank. 'We haven't seen him.'

'I thought he might be here,' said Thrale, brushing the snow from his face.

'What have you done to your cheek?' asked Frank.

'The Jerries came to the house. They were looking for the wireless.'

'Did they find it?'

Thrale shook his head. 'It wasn't there. Damned if I know where it was but it wasn't there. Leslie tried to divert them. He just ran off, the daft young devil. I thought he was heading this way. I'd better get back and see if he's come home.'

But the partisan leader barred his way. 'I can't allow that,' he said.

'What are you talking about?'

'You know about us. You're going to have to stay.'

'Am I now?' said Thrale.

'If you were picked up we'd all be in danger. I've no choice. And nor have you. Can you use a gun?'

'Yes,' said the keeper, 'yes, I can use a gun.'

'Take this one.'

Thrale took the rifle the partisan leader handed him. He held it for a moment, just looking at it.

'Are you sure you know how to use that?' said the partisan.

Thrale lifted the gun and registered its weight. Then he put it to his shoulder and, squinting along the barrel, adjusted the sight.

'Yes, I know how to use it,' he said calmly. 'I've been waiting three long years to do just that.'

'He thinks I told on you, Mrs Thrale. He thinks it was me told them where to look. You don't think that, do you?'

'No, dear; I don't think that.'

The tears ran down Mill's face and her shoulders rose and fell as she choked back the sobs. 'I can't bear to think of him thinking I done that; I can't.'

'He doesn't think that, Mildred. He knows you too well.'

'But he's been so angry with me. Ever since he saw us together. He said he didn't know who I was any more. That's what he said, Mrs Thrale. I'm his sister! We've been together all our lives. I can't bear to think of him thinking things like that about me.'

They stood together in the shelter of the trees not far from Thrales' cottage.

'And that was your friend—the soldier?' said Vera. 'The one who came with the search party?'

Mill nodded.

'I thought it must be from the way he looked at you.'

'I heard about what they was doing when I was down the shop. And then I saw Dieter was with them and . . . and I didn't know what to do. I didn't know what it was he did. He said he wasn't allowed to say. I didn't know he looked for wirelesses, not till this morning. I swear I never. Poor Dieter. But I couldn't let them find it, could I? Will he get into trouble now? I know he will! I've never been this unhappy, Mrs Thrale, not ever. What can I do?'

'What you did you did for the best. You did it to protect your friends despite what it might mean for someone you were fond of. That was very hard for you. And it was very brave of you. And Leslie was brave trying to distract their attention the way he did. We're all being brave, dear. And we have to go on being brave. No matter how unhappy we are. Give me the spade.'

Mill handed her the spade and Vera began to dig. 'You're quite sure this is the spot?' she asked.

Mill nodded. 'I couldn't go far. I didn't have time. I did it when I came back from the shop. You was upstairs.'

'You could have come and told me, you know.'

'I didn't know what to do. I was so confused seeing Dieter like that. I was afraid you'd think I . . . I was going to put it back if they didn't come. And then no one would have needed to know anything.'

'Poor Mildred. What an awful situation to be in.'

Vera lifted the samples case clear and brushed away the loose earth. 'I don't think it's come to any harm. Mr Crompton will be relieved.'

'What are we going to do?'

'Go back to the house. And wait.'

'For Mr Thrale?'

'Yes. And for Leslie too. Come along, dear. We've a lot of tidying up to do.'

'"Kansas Parker swallowed a last shot of red-eye and walked slowly to the door of the Ace of Spades Saloon. The tumbleweeds were shifting uneasily in the desert wind which stirred the dust along Main Street. There wasn't a soul to be seen. He was the only good hombre left in town.

"A train whistle wailed in the distance. The three-ten from Yuma. The train Clint Nolan and his pistoleros would be on. Kansas reached his pearl-handled six-shooter from its holster and spun the chamber. Then he took the sheriff's star from his pocket and pinned it to his shirt. He—"'

'Mr Crompton? Mr Crompton, are you there?'

Stan looked up from his book. Damn! 'Yes, I'm here, ladies,' he called. 'Come in.'

The Misses Elliott opened the door but remained on the landing outside. 'We're so sorry to bother you, Mr Crompton, but it's Mr Sims.'

'What about him?'

'He's not back yet,' said Miss Agnes.

'And the snow is falling so heavily,' said Miss Florence.

'He's probably taken shelter somewhere. I'm sure

there's nothing to worry about. And he was dressed for the bad weather.'

'If you say so, Mr Crompton.'

'But it is getting very close to tea-time.'

'He'll be back, ladies. You mustn't worry.'

But the ladies didn't seem convinced. And nor for that matter was Stan himself. He tried to return to the Ace of Spades Saloon and the few pages that remained: Nolan and his jailbirds were coming to reclaim Parker's Crossing and only Kansas Parker stood between them and the peace-loving town. But it wouldn't seem to hold him. Instead he stood by the window looking out at the whirling snowflakes. And wondering how the real battle had gone.

But not for long. The sound of Ilkley barking and of the old dears' bird-like voices twittering downstairs brought a smile to his lips. The professor was back! Well, that was a relief. He must go down and speak to him.

He heard the front-door opening; and it was as he was turning from the window that he caught sight of the figures in the garden below. There were two of them. And a large Alsatian dog.

And those shouts from the hall below: they certainly weren't the dear ladies or the professor.

He snatched up *The Sidewinder* and hurried across to the fire. He tore the pages from its flimsy spine and threw them into the flames. When he was sure they were burning he made his way to the bedside table, opened the bottle there and tipped two tablets into the palm of his hand. He was pouring water from the jug into his glass when Inspector Reiss and his men threw open the door.

'Herr Crompton?'

'The very same.'

'I have some questions I would like you to answer.'

'Anytime you like, old man.' Stan Crompton slipped the tablets into his mouth and raised his glass: 'Cheers,' he said.

Chapter 14

'Mr Thrale?'

'Frank?'

'Did Les say anything to you about me not wanting to fight?'

The keeper shook his head. 'I took it for granted you'd be going with him.'

'But he didn't tell me about it, Mr Thrale. Not a word. And he told the others that I . . . ' Frank shook his head.

'Something's been up with him,' said Thrale. 'He en't been himself this last week and more.'

'You're to cut out all the jawing,' said the partisan, who dropped down beside them. 'And that's an order. Sound carries.'

They watched him crawl back along the side of the ruined wall and take up his position with the machine-gun overlooking the road.

Thrale with his rifle, and Frank and Peter Sims with a small box of grenades, had been placed in what seemed to be a cellar nearby.

'It's part of the hypercaust system,' Sims had explained, as they climbed down into it. 'The under-floor heating system. The floor has collapsed, you see? Though it's still very impressive.'

Concealed under their white sheets they waited while the afternoon wore on. A watcher had been posted higher up the hill to give warning of the convoy's approach. Though there was little to see even from that vantage point as the snow fell faster and thicker and the light began to fade.

'D'you think they'll come?' whispered Frank.

Thrale shrugged. 'Whatever they do I don't like being up here with our back to the hill,' he said. 'We'd be stuck good and proper if something was to go amiss.'

'Retreating would certainly be a problem,' said Sims.

'P'raps we en't meant to retreat,' said Thrale.

'Ah!' Sims took off his hat and ran his fingers through his hair. 'Yes, I hadn't thought of that.'

'Mr Thrale!' said Frank, pulling at the keeper's sleeve. 'Look!'

The machine-gunner and the leader of the partisans had been joined by the watcher who had come down from the hill. And he was not alone.

'He was wandering about up top,' said the watcher.

The partisan leader took Les by his coat lapels and shook him angrily. 'What the hell do you think you're playing at?'

'I've come to help,' said Les.

'Come to get us killed more like.'

'Nobody saw me, I swear.'

'Well, we're stuck with you now. Get across to the others. And keep your head down. We've got no more sheets.'

Frank, Alec, and Mr Sims watched Les stoop and run quickly to their hiding place.

'Hello, Gill,' said Sims, as he dropped down into the cellar. 'We've been worried about you.'

'Frank?' said Les. 'How did you get here?'

'No thanks to you, Les.'

'Frank . . . Mr Thrale? What are you doing here?'

'I came looking for you, Leslie.'

'Mr Thrale, it was Mill's fault. It was her betrayed us to that German and his pals.'

'What are you saying?'

'It's the truth. She's been knockin' about with him. I should have told somebody before. It was Mill told 'em where to find the wireless.'

Thrale shook his head. 'I don't think so, Leslie. That's just it, you see,' he said, 'they didn't find it.'

'They must have. I mean, 'course they did. They must have.'

'No, Leslie. Because it wasn't there.'

'But Mrs Thrale and Mill hid it and . . . '

'I'm telling you, it wasn't there. And it weren't me that moved it. And I don't believe Vera did neither. She would have told me. And she was as feared as anyone else when those Nazis arrived.'

'Well, it wasn't me,' said Les. 'I didn't even know where it was. I . . . '

'Then there's only one person it could have been.'

'But . . . No. No,' he said, 'it can't have been Mill. She . . . I thought she . . . ' Les looked from one to the other and shook his head slowly from side to side.

In the silence, somewhere on the hill above them a single bird cawed hoarsely. Once. Twice. Three times.

'Listen!' said Sims. 'Isn't that the signal?'

The leader of the partisans came scrambling over the edge of the cellar.

'They're coming. You know what you have to do,' he said. 'Do that and nothing more. And you,' he said, pointing at Les, 'just keep your head down. Help the archaeologist with the grenades. Did you hear what I said?'

Les did not reply. He didn't even seem to be listening. He was sitting with his back to the wall staring in front of him.

The partisan turned to Alec. 'Wait for the green flare,' he said. 'We attack only then. Not a moment before. And from now on I want absolute silence.'

He climbed out of the cellar and crawled back to his place beside the machine-gun.

And then they heard it. The rumble of heavy trucks. The sound came and went on the gusting wind which tossed the snow in great flurries between the watchers and their prey. But there it was. And there, not long after, was the sudden sweep of headlights glaring through the snow as the scout vehicle led the first of the convoy round the turn in the road.

Thrale eased open the bolt on his rifle and peered along the sight.

Sims looked at Frank. 'Good luck,' he mouthed.

Then another gust of wind swept the sound of the trucks away and there was silence everywhere. A silence that was broken by a crackling noise somewhere over the wood. The flare burst high above the trees and all at once the landscape was bathed in light as it floated down slowly through the falling snow.

Everyone looked up. 'Good Lord!' said Sims. 'Good Lord, how beautiful! It's just like spring!'

And it was true, for a long moment the falling flare turned the snow-covered fields, the ruins, and the road to a spring-like green.

And then the machine-gun clattered into life.

The driver of the scout-car stamped on his brakes and it skidded to a halt slipping sideways across the road. There were shouts from the trucks and soldiers began to jump down desperately seeking cover and returning fire as they did so.

Alec was firing steadily down the hill. Careful, considered shots each of which dropped a grey-uniformed figure into the snow. The guns in the wood opposite now began to open up and there was confusion on the road below. In those first moments the partisans seemed to have the advantage.

But it was only for a moment.

There was a shout from the machine-gun position and Frank and Sims saw the gunner slump against the wall. The bearded leader dragged him to one side and took over the weapon.

'Give us a grenade, Mr Sims!' said Frank.

'Yes, of course,' said Sims.

He reached into the box and was about to hand a grenade to Frank when they saw one of the soldiers on the road below stand up and draw back his arm. Alec swung his rifle in his direction but even as he fired the soldier hurled the stick-bomb up the hill. It exploded with a deafening roar which sent snow and splintered stone in all directions.

When the smoke cleared they sat shaking their heads trying desperately to restore their hearing.

'Oh, no!' said Frank.

'Tate?' said Sims. 'What is it? Tate, are you all right?'

'Oh, no,' said Frank. 'Look what they've done.'

Nan's bicycle lay in a blackened star of earth where the stick-bomb had exploded; it was a tangled wreck and Frank's suitcase lay charred and torn beside it.

'They're coming up the hill!' yelled Thrale. 'Leslie, get over there and give him a hand with that machine-gun. Leslie, did you hear me?'

Les got slowly to his feet. Then without any warning he stooped and snatched a grenade from the box beside Sims. Before anyone could stop him he had scrambled over the rim of the cellar.

'Les!' yelled Frank.

But Les was on his feet and running down the hill. Without a sheet to cover him he was a sitting target. Frank saw him stumble and fall headlong. He was fumbling desperately with the grenade. His arm went up and tossed it towards the road but almost at the same time there was an explosion a few yards in front of him.

Frank clambered out of the cellar and ran to where he lay. 'Les? Les, are you hit?'

Les shook his head. 'I've done me ankle.'

There was another explosion close by and the smoke closed round them as clods of earth and fragments of brick and stone rained down. 'We're going to have to run for it,' said Frank. 'Grab hold of me.'

Half carrying and half dragging him, Frank hauled them both towards one of the nearby cellars. They tumbled in and lay among the rubble while bullets whined above them and ricocheted off the stone parapet.

Frank looked around their hiding-place. Shells had already blown away several large sections of the wall. 'They know we're here, Les. They saw us. We can't stay long.'

Les pulled down his sock painfully and inspected his ankle which was already beginning to swell.

'How bad is it?' said Frank.

'It don't half hurt.'

'We've got to get back to Sims and Mr Thrale.'

'Frank?'

'What?'

'Look, Frank . . . I never meant . . . I was angry, Frank, about you just going away like that. And about Mill and . . . and all of it.'

'It don't matter, Les.'

'It does. 'Course it does.'

'Les, the only thing that matters now is to get us out of here.'

'Leave me here.'

'Don't be daft.'

'They've got us pinned down. You might make it on your own.'

'Our machine-gun's still firing. Listen.'

Crouched behind the wall overlooking the road the partisan leader checked the emptying box of ammunition. 'We've got to get back up the hill,' he said.

His companion, who was bleeding heavily from a wound in his shoulder, nodded. 'They'll send men round behind us if we're not quick. Leave me the gun. I'll cover you as you move out.'

The partisan leader nodded. 'I'll tell the rest of them,' he said. And crawled away. 'Where's the other two?' he demanded, as he clambered down beside Thrale and Sims.

'Over yonder,' said the keeper, indicating the other cellar.

'What the hell are they doing there? Look, with covering fire we may make it up the gully and over the hill. We're going to have to move fast.'

'I'll warn them,' said Sims. He pulled his hat down over his eyes and sprinted for the cellar where the boys were. There were mortars exploding now on all sides. And the blast from one caught Sims as he reached the edge and propelled him over and down on to the rubble below. He staggered to his feet, dazed by the explosion.

'Mr Sims?'

'Ah, there you are,' he said, crawling to where Frank and Les were sheltering against the cellar wall. 'This is all getting rather dangerous, isn't it? We're going to try and retreat up the hill. I've come to issue you with an invitation. Do you think you can cope, Gill?'

'I don't know,' said Les.

'Well we ain't going to leave you here. Are we, Mr Sims? . . . Mr Sims?'

But Sims did not reply. He was staring at the blackened cellar wall to the right of where the boys were sitting.

'Good heavens!' they heard him say. 'Oh, good heavens!'

Frank turned to look. One of the mortar shells had blasted a large hole in the wall; the brickwork was broken all around the edge and there was a gaping area of darkness beyond. 'Sir, what's the matter? What is it?'

'It's . . . I'll tell you what it is, Tate—It is. It can't really be anything else. It must be! It's a cryptoporticus!' said the teacher.

'A what?'

Sims laughed. 'Dear God, Henry Underwood was right all the time! This *is* a palace; dear old Patfield is a palace, after all. It can't be otherwise. Only the very finest dwellings had such features. The palaces at Ostia and Herculaneum, places like that, the great palaces of the very rich indeed. Henry Underwood always believed . . . '

'But what is it?'

'It's a tunnel, Tate; an enclosed corridor that runs right under what would have been the portico!'

'Where does it go?'

'Straight on,' said Sims. 'Under where the road is now to the other side of the villa, of the palace!'

'Frank? Mr Sims?' Alec Thrale was calling. 'Are you all right? We can't wait much longer.'

'Mr Thrale, come at once,' called Sims. 'Over here. Quickly!'

'What're you playing at?' said Thrale, as he joined them in the cellar. 'That machine-gun can't hold them off much longer.'

'Mr Thrale, he's found a way out,' said Frank.

'A what?'

'There's a way out. Isn't there, Mr Sims?'

'I calculate it would have come out near the front of the villa which was over there towards the woods.'

'What would?'

'The crypto . . . the thing,' said Frank. 'There, in the wall.'

'It looks like a damn great hole to me.'

'No, Mr Thrale,' said Sims, 'it's a cryptoporticus. I'd stake my reputation on it. Has anyone got a light?'

Thrale took a box of matches from his pocket and handed them to the schoolmaster.

Sims struck one and, cupping his hand around the flame, he stepped through the hole and into the darkness beyond. As Sims disappeared inside another mortar landed close by scattering earth and bricks.

The leader of the partisans slid over the cellar's lip and hurried across to where they were huddled. 'They'll be all over us in a minute or two,' he said. 'We've got to move. Now. We've got to get up that hill.'

'We don't have to go up the hill,' said Alec calmly.

'Of course we do.'

'No. Sims reckons there's a way we can come up on the other side of them.'

'He reckons what?'

'He's in there now.'

'In where?' said the partisan, looking round the cellar.

'Mr Sims?' Frank called, standing at the entrance to the passageway. 'Mr Sims, are you all right?'

The answer came faintly from somewhere along the tunnel. 'Heavens, yes! It's all utterly beautiful.'

'In there?' said the partisan. 'We'd be caught like rats in a trap.'

'We already are, friend,' said Thrale. 'This is our only chance. I trust the schoolmaster. Come on.'

Frank helped Les to his feet and they followed Alec into the tunnel. The partisan leader hesitated for a moment and then plunged in after them.

The silence was immediate. As they moved forward blindly into what was soon absolute darkness it was as though a door had been closed behind them and the battle raging above might not have been happening at all.

'Mr Sims?' whispered Thrale. 'Mr Sims?'

But no reply came. Then, not far ahead of them, they saw the flame of a match burning steadily in the still air. The flame guttered and went out and another was struck and flared, lighting up a patch of the wall and Sims's face leaning forward intently.

'Look!' he said ecstatically. 'Just look at it!'

On the peeling plaster, faded and barely discernible by the tiny flame of the burning match, were faces: shadowy, distracted faces that seemed to contort as the flickering light moved backwards and forwards across the painted surface.

'What the hell is it?'

Sims laughed. 'Precisely! Isn't it obvious? It's the Underworld!'

'They look like . . . they look like the people I saw at Middelbury,' said Frank. 'Like ghosts.'

'They are ghosts, Tate; they're shades! Don't you see? This is the Realm of the Dead. This is where Proserpina comes each year. This is where she comes back from. Gill, you were right—don't you remember?'

Les shook his head.

'When you saw the photo of the Proserpina Floor? You

said you thought she looked as if she'd just stepped through a door. She had. She'd just stepped through the door from here. I'm willing to swear when we reach the end of this passage we'll come out on to the Proserpina floor!'

As Sims was speaking the tunnel shook and thin spirals of pale dust drifted down from among the figures and faces crowding the ceiling above.

'This lot's going to come in on us if we don't get a move on,' said Thrale.

But Sims had struck another match. 'Do you realize no one has seen these walls since the palace fell into decay fifteen hundred years ago,' he said. 'How superb! To have the Underworld swarming beneath your house. Don't you see? No ordinary building would have had something like this.'

Thrale pushed past him into the darkness beyond. They heard him moving along the tunnel. Then they heard him say: 'It's blocked. Come on, I need more hands.'

Frank, Les, and the partisan pushed past Sims and joined Alec at what seemed to be the end of the tunnel.

'Let's hope it's just fallen masonry,' said Thrale. And began pulling away at the stones. 'Pass them back,' he said. They formed a chain and began to pass the stones from hand to hand. Almost at once they felt cold air on their faces as gaps began to appear. Then with a rush of light which blinded them the stones fell away to reveal the snow-covered ruin on the other side.

Thrale peered out. 'We're about fifty yards from the wood,' he said. 'There's some cover within the ruin but after that it's open ground. We'll need covering fire. Where are they? Why is no one firing from the wood?'

The partisan leader shook his head. 'They'll have withdrawn,' he said. 'Those were my orders. They weren't meant to hang about. There won't be any covering fire.'

'Then God help us,' said Thrale.

'Is it? Is it the Proserpina floor?' called Sims. 'Was I right?' He pushed past them and out into the courtyard beyond the mouth of the tunnel. He knelt down and began to scrape away the snow. With each sweep of his hand a curve of the mosaic was revealed: a cornucopia of fruit, a sheaf of wheat, and finally the smiling face of the goddess herself. 'There she is!' he said. And turned to them. 'Now it all makes sense. Look at her! She's come back!'

'Leslie?' said Thrale. 'Can you run on that ankle?'

'I'll be helping him, Mr Thrale,' said Frank.

'No, you won't,' said Les. 'You'll get shot and all if you do.'

'Les, just shut up. Don't listen to him, Mr Thrale. Me and him will go together.'

'If we get separated,' said the partisan, 'keep going east and head for Elmshurst. Ask for Skelton's farm. We'll regroup there.'

'Why can't we go back to Shevington?' said Les.

'Not today, son. Not for a good many days. They'll come after us good and proper now. Nowhere will be safe, let alone the place where you live.' He looked round at them all. 'Well,' he said, 'it's not a thing I'm inclined to put my trust in normally but on this occasion I think we're going to need it: good luck.'

'We'll be hidden as far as that wall. You three wait here,' said Thrale. 'When it's safe to cross we'll tell you. And keep your heads down.'

Bent double Thrale and the partisan sprinted across the Proserpina floor to the far wall. They waited a moment and when no firing came they turned and beckoned to Frank and Les and Sims.

Frank helped Les to his feet. 'Fit?' he said. And Les nodded. 'Mr Sims?' Sims smiled. 'Come on, then.'

They set off through the snow and rubble until they reached the safety of the far wall where Alec and the partisan leader were waiting. It was only then that they realized that Sims wasn't with them. He had stopped halfway and was standing looking back towards the doorway of the tunnel.

'Sims!' called Thrale. 'Get down, man!'

'I shan't be a moment,' Sims replied. He raised his hat to the goddess smiling up from the snow beneath his feet. And then, as he was about to turn and make for the wall, a shot rang out.

'Mr Sims!' Frank ran back to where the teacher lay and Alec Thrale hurried after him. Peter Sims was curled up in the snow, his rakish trilby had fallen beside him. His right hand was raised as if to brush back his hair, the way he so frequently did. In fact his fingers were reaching for a neat, dark hole in his forehead.

'Oh, you silly beggar,' said Thrale quietly.

Frank turned to the keeper. 'Is he . . . '

'Help me pull that sheet off him. Quickly!'

'But, Mr Thrale . . . '

'He doesn't need it, Frank; and it might just give Leslie a chance. He's a sitting duck otherwise.'

They pulled the white sheet from the dead teacher. Then Thrale picked up his hat from the snow and placed it gently over his face. 'Come on,' he said to Frank. 'Time's running out.'

They hurried back to where Les and the partisan were waiting.

'Put this on, Leslie,' said Thrale, handing him the sheet. 'Lively now!'

'But what about Mr Sims?'

Frank shook his head. 'Put it on, Les.'

Les pulled the white cloak over his head. Then they all four sat listening. The gunfire had stopped. The Jerries were obviously waiting for them to break cover.

'Well,' said Thrale, 'they're not going to go away, are they. Time to make a move. Into the wood, right?'

The others nodded.

'Count of three and run like you've never run before! Leslie, are you ready?'

Les nodded.

'One. Two. Three!'

The four white-robed figures rose from the cover of the wall, and, as the enemy rifles began to fire, stumbled forward into the swirling curtain of snow.

AFTERMATH

Like so many districts in London, Clerkenwell still bore the scars of the long days and nights of remorseless bombing which had preceded the invasion. Craters still gaped in the roads; and wherever you looked along the terraced streets there were scorched ruins and desolate oases of wasteland where only weeds and broken walls seemed to grow.

The young man in the threadbare overcoat looked up at the housefronts as he passed. He wore a battered trilby hat and carried a haversack over his shoulder.

Despite the summer sunshine the street had a grey, neglected air, like an old shelf left to gather dust. But its pavements were busy enough. Housewives stood gossiping on the steps, and on the pavements below there were mothers with prams and small children clinging to their skirts. There was no passing traffic, and the only sound was the sound of the children playing in the road: some boys kicking a football made of newspapers tied with string, and six or seven girls in a long line waiting to duck in under the slowly turning skipping-rope.

The young man had almost reached the end of the street when the car appeared. It drove slowly along the kerb and stopped not far from the corner. Two of the Gestapo agents who got out took one side of the street and two the other. The children playing in the road seemed used to these alarms and didn't even stop to watch.

The young man found himself ushered into a line next to the railings.

'What are they looking for?' he asked.

'Anything at all, pal,' the man in front replied. 'They've been arresting people left, right, and centre recently.'

The young man took out his papers ready for inspection.

The line moved forward quickly and he soon found himself facing a burly figure in a leather coat. The Gestapo officer looked him up and down. 'These your papers?' he said. He was English.

The young man nodded.

'Sampson? Eric Sampson? Is that your name?'

'That's right.'

The agent held the identity-card to the light and squinted at it. 'And what are you doing in London, Mr Sampson?'

'I'm looking for work.'

'Take your hat off.' The young man did so and the agent shook his head. 'It says here that you're eighteen. You're never eighteen,' he said. 'Wait.' He handed him the card and gestured towards the railings.

Eric Sampson felt his mouth go dry. But he did as he was told. He put on his hat and waited quietly while the queue moved forward. Half a dozen people, no more. When they had been checked, or perhaps before, he would have to make a move. His fingers felt deep in the pocket of his overcoat and released the safety-catch on the pistol concealed there.

Which was when the shouting began. It came from one of the nearby streets. And suddenly grew louder as a horse and cart came careering round the corner. The driver was struggling frantically to regain control of the runaway animal but, as it turned, one of the wheel-hubs struck a lamp-post and tipped the cart on to its side. Its twisted load of scrap-metal cascaded into the road close to the Gestapo agents' car. The driver picked himself up and hurried across to the horse which was kicking for all it was worth, trapped among the traces and broken shafts.

The Gestapo men ran to their vehicle and began to pull away the debris. No one watching made any effort to help them. Instead, a small crowd formed around the young man by the railings.

'Leg it, son,' said an old woman quietly. 'While the going's good.'

He didn't wait to be told twice. If the last months had taught him anything at all it was that: don't wait a moment longer than you have to. Screened from view by the crowd he slipped round the corner and made off into the labyrinth of streets beyond.

It took another five anxious minutes to find the address he was looking for: Salisbury Street. Number fifty-seven was a sombre, three-storeyed house. He went up the steps and knocked. After a while a young woman came to the door.

'Yes?' she said.

'Is this Doctor Freeman's surgery?' he asked.

'Whatever makes you think that?'

He hesitated. 'This is the address they gave me. The hospital sent me.'

'Which hospital?'

'St Hereward's.'

'I think there must be some mistake,' she said. 'You'd better come in for a moment.'

He stepped inside and she closed the door behind him. She then disappeared into a room at the back of the house leaving him alone in the hallway.

Had he got the address wrong? Surely that was what they'd said: 57, Salisbury Street? He'd memorized it carefully. But if this wasn't the right place . . .

The young woman had left the door slightly ajar and he was sure someone came to look at him through the gap. Again he slipped his hand into his pocket and his fingers closed around the weapon hidden there. And, as he did, the door was thrown open and Les Gill came hurrying out.

'Bloody hell, Frank, we've been worried sick!' he said. 'We've been expecting you since yesterday.'

'Give us a chance, Les. This is a big city.'

Frank followed his friend into the back room. Sitting at a table was an elderly man and standing beside him was the young woman who had opened the door. Sitting on a large sofa nearby was Alec Thrale. He got up as Frank came in. 'Hello, Frank,' he said.

'Mr Thrale. When did you get here?'

'Last night. Les and me travelled together.'

'First things first,' said the young woman. 'I expect you're hungry. I can do you some toast. Would that be acceptable?'

'Yes, please,' said Frank.

'Do sit down. I'm sure you're exhausted. I'm Emily Marlowe, by the way. And this is my father. And you are?'

'Frank, Frank Tate.'

'And is that the name on your papers, Mr Tate?' Mr Marlowe enquired.

'Oh, no,' said Frank. 'No, that's Eric, Eric Sampson.'

'Then I think that's what we'd better stick to, don't you?'

'I'm Raymond Tulliver,' said Les.

'And I'm Percy,' Alec Thrale said dourly, 'Percy Gilbert. Though I don't feel like a Percy or much of a Gilbert either.'

The boys laughed. But Mr Marlowe didn't seem to find it funny.

'I'm afraid our identities are one of the sacrifices we are required to make, Mr Gilbert,' he said. 'We are at war.'

'I know that,' said Alec. 'I'm just saying—'

But Marlowe interrupted him. 'And this time we are going to win.'

Frank sat forward in his chair. He could feel the tiredness getting the better of him. 'How was your journey, Les?' he asked. The three of them had parted not far from Guildford almost a week before. From there Frank had been on his own. Living on his nerves. Constantly looking over his shoulder. Passed from one group to another until, on the outskirts of London, he had been handed his new identity and the address of the safe house in Salisbury Street. Les and Alec began to tell him their story. But the presence of his friends, the warmth of the room, and the welcome sense of safety finally overwhelmed him; his head dropped on to his chest and he was asleep within minutes.

'Let him sleep,' said Mr Marlowe. 'And you'd be wise to snatch a few hours yourselves. They may come for you tonight.'

'What do you mean?' said Thrale.

'There are lorries that go north from the markets. From Covent Garden and Smithfields. It's all quite legitimate. Except that some of their load isn't always quite what it claims to be.'

Emily Marlowe returned with a plate of toast. 'Poor boy,' she said, looking down at Frank's sleeping figure. 'He was exhausted.'

Her father nodded. 'I think we'll leave all our guests to get some rest,' he said.

'You said we might go north?' said Alec, as Marlowe rose from the table.

'I imagine that's the direction you'll take.'

'To where the fighting is?' asked Les.

Mr Marlowe did not reply.

'How far north?' said Thrale. 'Do you know that?'

'I'm afraid not, Mr Gilbert. Beyond the front door of this house your journey is not my concern. By the way, I'll try to give you warning when the time comes but when it does it's vital you're ready to leave at a moment's notice.'

Father and daughter went out.

'What do you reckon, Mr Thrale?' said Les.

'Mr Gilbert,' said the keeper. 'I reckon we ought to do just what he said and try and get some sleep.'

Thrale pulled a cushion behind his head and closed his eyes.

But Les stayed awake. The first thing he did was to wrap the toast in a piece of paper and slip it into

Frank's bag. Then he sat at the end of the sofa watching his companions.

Everything had changed, hadn't it?

Frank would never find his dad now.

And Mr Thrale? It was Alec Les felt most sorry for. Alec hadn't even wanted to join the partisans. Though once he had there were few cooler or more determined fighters than Alec Thrale. Alec had had to leave so much behind. Everything really. And because they weren't allowed to contact anybody Vera wouldn't even know what had happened to him. Nobody knew what had happened to any of them.

And for himself? What had changed for Les Gill . . . the one who'd wanted to fight, to pay the Jerries back for what they'd done?

And he remembered her face turning to look at him. There was hardly a day when that face didn't turn and look at him. Hardly a day when the soldiers didn't come bursting through the Thrales' door and that young Jerry with them. Hardly a day when his sister didn't turn to him with that terrible look. The look she gave him when she saw what he thought she'd done.

'Sorry, Mill,' he said quietly.

Then he curled up at the end of the sofa and tried to sleep. When the time came the important thing was to be ready. Ready to fight. That was all there was left to do.

Also by Michael Cronin

Against the Day

ISBN 0 19 275039 9

Shortlisted for the Angus Book Award

'Cronin's novel of occupation is written with a strong feel for the historical moment . . . this is a gripping and enjoyable first novel with a strong sense of uneasy and menacing times'

Books for Keeps

'A solidly crafted plot builds to a well-hidden surprise at its climax'

Daily Telegraph

'This is a tale that is thrilling and chilling at the same time and will also undoubtedly prove enjoyable to history buffs. Realistically constructed, with Cronin paying meticulous attention to character development, it is also a disturbing tale that, had the fates played a different hand, would have been even more realistic than it is. Well written and intensely gripping'

School Librarian

From *Against the Day*

Chapter 1

'Look at you!'

'What?' Colin had just come in from out-the-back and was struggling with his braces.

'You look wore out before you start.'

'I can't sleep, ma,' he said. 'I've told you that before. Not with Frank in the room.'

Edie Worth took the comb from the mantelpiece and began to drag it through her son's hair. 'What's he done now?' she said.

'He's making noises again.'

'Dreaming?'

'Talking to himself. Ow!' Colin pulled away, rubbing the top of his head. 'He keeps me awake, ma. It's not fair.'

'There's plenty that's not fair in this world, my lad. The sooner you realize that the happier you'll be. Now get yourself off to school.'

'What about Frank?'

'If Frank Tate wants to be late for school that's his look-out.'

When Colin had gone Edie put her hand to the pot. It was still warm—just. As she sat and sipped the dark tea she looked around the room: the big old range, the rods of washing hung above it to dry, the glass-fronted cabinet crammed with her mother's bits and pieces of china, and the sink that was always full these days—like the cottage itself. And she tried to picture her own kitchen in the poky terraced house in Swindon. It wasn't much but it had been hers. And Len's. Still would be if it hadn't been for the blessed war. Now her husband was a prisoner of war somewhere in France she couldn't even pronounce and she was back in the cottage in Shevington where she'd been born. It wasn't fair.

There were footsteps on the stairs and Frank pushed open the door and sat down at the table.

'Good morning, Auntie Edie,' she said caustically.

'Morning.'

She watched him as he spread his bread with marge. He was the same age as Colin, they'd been born within a couple of months of each other. But that was where the likeness ended. Frank Tate was spoilt. Her brother Bill had ruined his only son. What with that and the life the two of them had led, hand to mouth, never in the same place six months at a time, rooms and boarding-houses, it was little wonder he was such a handful.

'You been dreaming again?'

'No,' he said, and folded his bread into a sandwich. But he had. In his dream—it was the one he'd had before—he had been out looking for his dad. All over Seabourne, all along the seafront, on the pier, up the High Street. Then, as he was crossing the Municipal Bowling Green, he saw the old macintosh, the one just like his dad used to wear, lying in the gully at the edge of the neatly-trimmed grass. Just an old mac. Until he went closer and saw the slippered feet and pyjama trousers. It wasn't his dad; it was an old man. He had never seen a dead person before but he knew that that was what he was: he had a discarded look, just as though someone had thrown him away. His panama hat lay next to him. There was a dark, oval bruise on his temple. His eyes were open and were glaring accusingly at the big, white pebble on the grass beside his head. There were pebbles everywhere.

'You kept Colin awake,' said his aunt.

'No I never.'

That was his father! That was her brother Bill all over. The first thing Bill Tate always did was deny it—

whatever it was. 'Yes, you did, my lad! And you know it. You were chattering away half the night.'

Frank picked up his slice and headed for the door.

'And where do you think you're going?'

'School.'

'You're going to get that copper lit for me before you do. I've got a basket of laundry to start the minute I've finished this mouthful of tea.'

The third match got the newspaper spills to light but it wasn't much of a flame. He'd be late again. She was always finding chores for him to do last thing. Anything to make his life a misery.

The checkpoint on the village green was unpredictable: that was the point, of course. You never knew when they'd stop you. And Frank was relieved as he came running down the lane to see that the barrier was raised. But then, as he approached, the guard—the one they called 'Bumpsadaisy'—stepped from the sentries' hut and held up his hand.

Frank pulled out his Identity Card and waited. The soldier frowned at it, comparing the photograph with the boy, the way he always did.

'You are twelve years old,' he said. 'I have a boy like you. He is twelve years old.'

But Frank said nothing. He never did.

'Bumpsadaisy' turned to his companions in the hut. '*Dieser, der mag uns nicht*,' he said. And Hans and 'Knees' laughed. 'You don't like us,' he said, bringing his face close to Frank's. But Frank didn't budge. The soldier shook his head. 'You are very stubborn,' he said, handing back the card. 'And you are late for school, I think.'

Warden Firth put down her thick blue pencil and stretched her aching fingers. There was always so much to be done. And these days it always had to be done: 'At once!' But that was the way SS Hauptsturmführer

Honegger liked things done. The Head of Security at Shevington Hall—Head of Security! And he couldn't be more than thirty, if that—was not a man with time to spare. She looked out at the garden beyond her window. It had to be confessed, it had a rather neglected air. But it couldn't be helped. There were more important things in her life now than tidy borders and rose cuttings.

Betty Firth had volunteered for the position of Village Warden because, as she had told the meeting summoned to the village hall within days of the Germans arriving, 'I love Shevington. And I want us to get back to normal as quickly as possible. I'm convinced it can be done and done without any unpleasantness. The authorities,' she had turned to acknowledge politely the Wehrmacht officer and his colleague with whom she shared the platform, 'have drawn up the rules by which we can do so. I want to play my part, ladies and gentlemen. You all know me and know I will always do so to the very best of my ability.'

They did all know her. She had always been a busybody. And now the Jerries had given her an armband and a telephone in her back sitting room to make it official. Now she had the right—and more power than even poor old Dick Carr, the village bobby—to be nosy. And she could always be counted on to be so to the very best of her ability.

In the kitchen she poured boiling water over the gauze bag of camomile flowers and watched the water colour in the bottom of the cup.

Back to normal. More or less. Six months, that was all it had taken. And it had been achieved with remarkable ease. One heard such horrid stories from elsewhere of what the Invasion and Occupation had brought. But Shevington had weathered the storm. There had been changes, that was inevitable. One or two new faces, of course. Edith Tate, Worth as she was now, was back at her mother's with her children: the boy, and the older girl who worked up at the Hall. The father, not a local man, had been captured at Dunkirk. Yes, Nan Tate certainly had a houseful what with the Worths and that other grandson of hers, the one who'd been orphaned: Bill Tate's son.

There had been losses, of course. But thankfully things hadn't lasted long enough for there to be too many. The two younger Cowdrey brothers. And Henry Underwood, the headmaster's son. And Tom Barlow—he'd lost an arm. It was very sad but it didn't do to dwell on such things. What else was there of note? Well, there were those two guttersnipes out at Keeper Thrale's. So typical of Vera Thrale to take in a pair like that: the big, pasty-faced girl and her runt of a brother. Gill was their name. Incorrigible cockney types. Products of the darkest East End.

Betty took her cup and went back into the office. While she was away the cat, Gargery, had slipped through the open window and was curled up in the big, wheel-backed chair opposite her desk.

The pile of letters to be censored had diminished appreciably since her early start that morning. At first she'd felt rather awkward listening to her neighbours' correspondence—that was how she thought of it: she knew them all so well she could hear their voices as she read them. But, finally, she'd come to the conclusion that wardenship demanded a certain detachment; and that whining and ill-considered remarks about the authorities didn't help the situation and did call for constant monitoring. And, in time, she was able to wield her blue indelible pencil without hesitation.

She sat down at her desk again. But before resuming her duties, she opened the envelope marked CONFIDENTIAL COMMUNICATION and re-read the letter which had arrived from the Hall earlier that morning. SECRET, it said at the top. And was signed by General von Schreier himself, the man in charge of the whole of the Southern Area Command. As a child Betty had always loved secrets; they were dangerous and demanding; but it was so nice to be trusted. When she'd finished, she slipped the letter back in its envelope and locked it carefully in the drawer of her desk. It would never do for unauthorized eyes to read it.

'That would spoil the surprise, wouldn't it, Gargery?' she said. And the cat blinked back at her.

Besides, everyone would know soon enough. The announcement would be made public in a couple of days. Such a surprise. And there would be so much to do. Still, forewarned was forearmed.

From the framed photograph above the desk Adolf Hitler's demanding gaze met hers.

'Getting on,' she said.

And picking up her pencil she went back to work.

The Gills, Les and Mill, had arrived in Shevington not long after Frank Tate. During the confused weeks that followed the Invasion the roads had been crowded with refugees, and no one had taken much notice when the ragged boy and girl came trudging along the Patfield Road pushing their battered pram. They had walked right through the village and were not far from the Hall when they stopped at Keeper Thrale's.

When General von Schreier made Shevington Hall his private residence, Sir Quentin Demeger had gone north to one of his family's estates in Derbyshire. But Sir Quentin's staff had stayed. What else was there to do? Most of them had worked at the Hall all their lives. Alec Thrale had walked its woods and fields as long as he could remember.

When Vera Thrale opened the door she saw a big, strong girl with a plain, honest face, who looked about fifteen years old and who certainly wasn't 'village'—her husband would never have allowed anyone from the village in the house—and a small boy with a mop of unruly black hair. Mill and Les saw a tall young woman wearing a threadbare silk dressing-gown secured at the waist with a man's tie.

'Any chance of a drink of water, missis?' asked Mill.

'You're from London!' said Vera, smiling.

'Yes,' said Mill.

'You look exhausted.'

'I ain't, but he is,' said Mill quickly. 'He's my brother.'

'Come inside.'

And that was it. Mill was given a bed in the attic; and Les a mattress and blankets in the shed across the yard.

It was where he and Frank retreated most evenings to lick their wounds among the battered suitcases and rusting garden-tools. Frank had spent ten minutes after school that afternoon trying to explain to Miss Meacher that it was his Aunt Edie who had made him late again. He was still doing so.

'I told her, Les,' he said. 'I told her it was Edie's fault.'

'Wasting your breath, Frank,' his friend replied. 'You ought to know that by now.'

'I know.' Frank sat down on the battered suitcase at the end of Les's mattress. 'Les?'

'What?'

Frank sighed. 'Oh, I don't know.'

'Don't take no notice—I don't.'

'Edie, Miss Meacher, all of 'em, they're always having a go at me. What's the matter with people?'

'People do—they like having a go at each other.'

'But it's worse now; it's worse since the Jerries came. Haven't you noticed that? People are arguing with each other all the time.'

'Keep your head down—that's what you want to do. I do.'

He did. Which was peculiar for someone who looked like a really tough nut. It was the one thing Frank found hard to cope with where Les was concerned. In every other way they were the best of friends. At first it was being outsiders that had thrown them together. Neither of them being particularly welcomed by the village kids. Then, as the months passed, they became inseparable. Two of a kind. But when it came to speaking up or having a go Les couldn't have been more unlike Frank.

'The fact is, Les, people didn't ought to be arguing with each other,' Frank said impatiently. 'The only ones people ought to be arguing with are the Nasties.'

Les shook his head. 'Leave off, eh! Only mugs argues with the Nasties. You fancy seeing off that white-haired geezer up at the Hall, do you—the SS Nasty? Don't be silly!'

The door from the yard opened and Mill Gill came in and closed it quickly behind her.

''Lo, Frank,' she said.

''Lo, Mill.'

She sat down on an upturned box and took a crumpled cigarette from the pocket of her apron. 'What're you looking so miserable about?' she said.

'Everything,' said Frank.

'Oh, is that all.' She lit the cigarette and inhaled luxuriously. 'Me and Vera's been spring-cleaning,' she said. 'Here! She was only dancing in the kitchen, wasn't she! With a feather duster. Never a dull moment with Vera.'

'What was she dancing for?'

Mill laughed. 'She says you don't need a reason. And what's the matter with you, Les? You look like you lost a pound and found a tanner.'

Frank and Les watched her as she tried very carefully to blow a smoke-ring. It didn't work; it never did. 'One of these days,' she said. 'Oh, cheer up, you two, for heaven's sake; you look a right pair of Jonahs.'

'It's this place,' said Frank. 'It's just Shevington and everything.'

'You don't know when you're well off, neither of you. There's plenty would be grateful living in a place like this.'

'Come off it, Mill. Nothing ever happens here. Nobody ever does anything!'

'What's people supposed to do, then—according to Frank Tate?'

'I don't know. Pay them back for a start.'

'Pay who back?'

'The Jerries, who else? Do something to . . . I don't know.'

'Listen to it! You want your bloody head read, you do. Do what, then?'

'Something. Not just sit back and let them do what they like. Like the night the soldiers took Cec Warwick and his family away. Yes, and burned their caravan. Remember that? Cos they was gypsies. What about that? Nobody did anything about that. Nobody even talks about it any more.'

'They took 'em away somewhere to re-settle 'em. They said so.'

'They burned their caravan, Mill! And smashed everything. My gran said Cec and his family been travelling these roads for years. People knew them, Mill. But nobody said anything or tried to help them. They just let the Jerries do it to them. That's what I mean.'

'Look, Frank,' said Mill, 'people's took a hammering. They just want a quiet life.'

'But if nobody ever does anything, Mill, it's . . . it's like they've won.'

'Who?'

'The Jerries!'

'Gawd, Frank—they *have* won!'

Frank shrugged. 'Still don't mean . . . look, it don't mean we can't go on hoping.'

'Here we go again.'

'Consider Garibaldi!'

'You and your Garibaldi! What's Garibaldi got to do with it?'

'Because Garibaldi never gave up.' It had been not long after Frank arrived at Nan Tate's, not long after he'd told her about his dad and everything, that his grandmother had pointed to the picture on the wall by the kitchen door: the big, bearded man with the red shirt, his arms folded, gazing steadfastly into the sun. Always consider Garibaldi, Frank, she'd told him; I set great store by that picture. That was your grandfather's picture. He'd thought she meant it was a picture of his grandfather and had asked her if Garibaldi was an Irish name. No, she said, it was Italian; Garibaldi was Italian. He'd found out the rest by sneaking a look at Colin's encyclopaedia, the one his cousin didn't allow anyone else to look at: 'Guiseppe Garibaldi, 1807–1882, patriot, soldier, and fighter for freedom'. He'd been captured, condemned to death, escaped, captured again, loads of times. Italy, South America, Italy again. And Garibaldi had never given up; he just kept going. But, then, you only had to look at his face to see that. 'It's a fact, Mill. Garibaldi never gave up hoping and I ain't either.'

'People want a quiet life and you can't blame them. Be fair, Frank.'

'Why?'

'Cos you have to be, that's why.'

'I don't know about that.'

'I do then. And there's something else I know: if you go looking for trouble them Nazis'll give it you, good and proper!'

'I know that.'

'You don't—you don't know when you're well off. I told you, there's plenty would be grateful living somewhere as quiet as this place. I am. And you are, ain't you, Les?'

'Leave off, Mill, eh? He only said—'

'Look, Mill,' said Frank, 'all I'm saying is you can't help . . . you can't help hoping, wanting something to happen, that's all.'

Mill stood up; she knew that when Frank Tate was in one of his Garibaldi moods there was no shifting him. 'I daresay,' she said, pinching the end from her cigarette and putting it back in the pocket of her pinny. 'Well, some of us have got work to do. Vera will be wondering where I am. Ta-ta. And just you behave yourselves.'

'Not much else we can do, is there?' said Frank.